A Canyon Springs Courtship

Glynna Kaye

⟨H⟩ HARLEQUIN® LOVE INSPIRED®

Recycling programs
for this product may
not exist in your area.

™ LOVE INSPIRED BOOKS

ISBN-13: 978-0-373-81718-4

A CANYON SPRINGS COURTSHIP

Copyright © 2013 by Glynna Kaye Sirpless

www.LoveInspiredBooks.com

Printed in U.S.A.

"Remember these are real people with real lives. They aren't striving to catch the world's eye."

"But isn't that why the town competed to have me come here?" Her lips twitched in an amusement that belied the tightness in her throat. "My blog puts forgotten little places in the limelight."

"All I'm asking is that you not exploit anyone. I think you owe me that."

Her breath caught. "I did the right thing."

"Keep telling yourself that, Macy."

She strengthened her grip on the purse in her lap. "I'm a journalist. What we're called to share with the public doesn't always make us feel great."

His firm jaw clenched. "I see."

But he didn't. He never had. If she could go back in time, maybe she'd handle the situation differently. Or maybe she wouldn't. A man who couldn't support her career choice wasn't the man for her.

"You're not to tell anyone we knew each other previously," he continued. "Understand?"

Not a request, a demand. She could only nod her response, also preferring no one knew she shared a past with this hard-hearted, mulish man.

Books by Glynna Kaye

Love Inspired

Dreaming of Home
Second Chance Courtship
At Home in His Heart
High Country Hearts
Look-Alike Lawman
A Canyon Springs Courtship

GLYNNA KAYE

treasures memories of growing up in small Midwestern towns—in Iowa, Missouri, Illinois—and vacations spent in another rural community with the Texan side of the family. She traces her love of storytelling to the many times a houseful of great-aunts and great-uncles gathered with her grandma to share hours of what they called "windjammers"—candid, heartwarming, poignant and often humorous tales of their youth and young adulthood.

Glynna now lives in Arizona, and when she isn't writing she's gardening and enjoying photography and the great outdoors.

Do nothing out of selfish ambition or vain conceit, but in humility consider others better than yourselves. Each of you should look not only to your own interests but also to the interests of others.
—*Philippians* 2:3–4

If the Son sets you free, you will be free indeed.
—*John* 8:36

To Helen Blackburn, my longtime "kindred spirit" and prayer warrior, whose faithfulness to God and to our friendship continues to inspire me.
Thank you.

Chapter One

Now he'd done it. He'd unthinkingly stuck his nose smack into Macy Colston's business. The last thing he had any intention of doing.

Standing next to the high-backed booth at Kit's Lodge and Restaurant, Jake Talford stared down at Macy's upturned face, barely noticing the teenage girl seated across from her who slipped from the booth and headed to the door, no doubt cowed by his stern expression.

In spite of himself, he hungrily searched Macy's delicate, winsome features. The flawless skin he knew to be satiny smooth under his fingertips. The subtle blush caressing high cheekbones. Expressive green eyes. But what was he searching for? Evidence that the still-appealing countenance no longer masked the relentless ambition he'd come to know too well?

"Macy," he said with a nod of acknowledgment, keeping his voice low. His heart hitched as he hurtled back in time six years to when he'd last seen the aspiring journalist. Back to the pain that had all but cracked open his heart—just like the ring box he'd flung across the room that day.

Her eyes narrowed slightly, but he didn't miss the fleeting alarm that shot through them. She wasn't any happier to see him than he was to see her.

"What are you doing in Canyon Springs, Jake?" Her soft, well-remembered voice held an edge, almost as if she suspected he'd stalked her to this small Arizona mountain community.

"I live here." He raised a brow at her blank look. "Surprised? Slacking on research isn't your customary style."

Her long-lashed eyes not leaving his, she licked her lower lip in an almost nervous gesture. His grip tightened on the Windbreaker jacket fisted in his hand. Macy? Nervous? Since when?

"I thought you were from Phoenix."

"Born there. Didn't stay there." But he didn't intend to rehash his history now. He motioned to the empty seat across from her. "Your friend is gone. Does that mean you're finished here?"

"I—"

"Good." Even though the Saturday lunchtime crowd was relatively sparse this time of year, he didn't care to have an audience for the conversation they needed to have. He dropped a twenty next to her coffee mug. "Then let's take this elsewhere, shall we?"

For a moment she hesitated, as if she feared leaving the rustic restaurant's dining room might not be a wise move. Then with a toss of her long, honey-blond hair she cast him a self-assured smile and gracefully rose. With a swirl of her floral sundress, she preceded him to the lobby. He moved to hold open the door and together they stepped onto the wooden-planked front porch. A bitter wind and a flurry of snowflakes greeted them.

April in the high country.

He took a step toward the parking lot. "My SUV's this way."

She didn't budge. "Where are we going?"

"Where the whole town won't hear what I have to say."

An amused half smile surfaced, reminding him of the many times he'd deliberately said and done things to provoke it, an excuse to kiss it from her lips. What a fool he'd been.

"In case you haven't noticed, Jake, I'm not wearing boots."

He glanced down at sandaled feet peeping from beneath the flowing cotton sundress, then shook his head.

"When I left Phoenix this morning," she enlightened him, "it was to be an eighty degree day. While your chamber of commerce sang the praises of a four season, higher-than-Denver elevation, nobody breathed a word about packing a parka and mukluks in April."

He thrust his Windbreaker into her hands. "Put this on. Then wait here. I'll get the truck."

Aware of her sharp gaze focused on his back, he strode across the graveled parking lot, two inches of snow crunching under his Western boots. He thrust his hand into his trouser pocket, searching for the miniature cross that had once been his grandfather's. He'd taken to carrying it as Granddad had, finding that the sensation of the smooth, seashell surface sliding between his fingers somehow grounded him. It reminded him not only that God was in control, but that he needed to measure up to the example his grandfather had set for him. And that meant not letting his temper get the better of him.

It was bound to happen, though, this running into Macy. He'd known she was expected, and in a town with a population of just under three thousand, he wouldn't have been able to avoid her forever. But on her first day of a monthlong assignment while he was dining with a client? He hadn't been ready for that.

He should have had the foresight to contact Macy in private before her arrival. Truth be told, he hadn't been thinking proactively, only hoped she'd get in and out of town before she even knew he called Canyon Springs home.

So much for that strategy.

Jake climbed into his vehicle and glanced back at the two-story log cabin lodge. Macy, chin lifted obstinately, still stood on the porch, his jacket folded primly in her crossed arms. He had to hand it to her for not turning on a dainty heel and marching back into the building after he'd almost strong-armed her from it. But then, she always had gumption.

Memory flashed to the day they'd first met. She'd stood almost exactly like that at a Missouri estate sale, the spark in her beautiful eyes daring him to outbid her. Even though he hadn't cared about the chair, he'd dragged the bidding out as long as he could, wanting to keep her attention on him A practicing attorney's funds trumped the ponytailed undergrad's budget. But when immediately afterward he'd offered to sell the antique office chair to her for a dollar, she'd given him a sassy grin and said she wasn't interested in the chair…just the bidder.

Pushing the memory away, he grabbed the leather briefcase and loose papers from the passenger side bucket seat and tossed them in the back, then started the SUV. With the windshield wipers in motion, he glanced again in Macy's direction.

"Lord," he muttered under his breath. "What are You thinking bringing her here?"

Sitting in the high-backed booth directly behind her a short while ago, their backs to each other, he'd recognized her voice before he'd seen her. When his client departed he remained frozen in place, lingering to listen to her interactions with those around her. As a professional blogger with the popular site *Hometowns With Heart,* Macy had an uncanny knack for ferreting out tasty personal tidbits to liven up her posts. She had put those skills to good use today. But this was his town. His people. He wouldn't allow her to take advantage of them for the sake of boosting her blog's popularity.

"Give me the right words. I don't want to start a war."

When he pulled the SUV to a stop in front of the lodge, Macy stepped forward as if impervious to the snow and whipping wind. Once inside, she shut the door, laid her purse on her lap and fastened her seat belt. Then she carefully placed his unused jacket on the console between them.

Still stubborn.

He bumped up the heat a notch, knowing she'd never ask him to, then drove toward the parking lot's exit and down the wet, hard-topped street. Casey Lake seemed a suitable destination. Or he'd drive clear to Albuquerque if that's what it took to make the situation clear to her.

But why'd she have to smell so good? Fresh. Citrusy. Just as he remembered.

"So what's on your mind, Jake?"

He remembered that, as well. Even at twenty-two she'd been direct. Confident. Not easily cowed. Not that he wanted to intimidate her now, just get her to understand—and agree—that breaking confidences shared by community residents was outside the boundaries of her invitation to feature Canyon Springs in her blog.

A quick glance in her direction confirmed that the initial signs of nervousness when he'd caught her off guard had vanished. Her countenance, even lovelier than it had been years ago, remained unruffled. Reminding himself not to get distracted, he tightened his hands on the steering wheel.

"I managed to keep out of it when your waitress related the story of her courtship. It might not be something her husband would want broadcast, but it's nothing the town doesn't already know."

Macy shifted in her seat, but didn't interrupt.

"And Reuben Falkner," he continued as they passed by towering ponderosa pines dusted with snow, "he can be a cantankerous old guy, so as far as I'm concerned, he's on his own. But when sweet, notoriously naive Chloe Bancroft started to shoot off her mouth about her equally sweet and notoriously naive stepmother, well—"

Macy gave a soft gasp.

"Are you suggesting I set her up to disclose private family matters to share in my blog?"

"You led her down a breadcrumb-strewn path," he said, keeping his tone firm. "Skillfully, I might add. You haven't lost your touch."

Her lips tightened. "I never set you up, Jake."

Still sticking to that lame story, was she?

"Ah, Macy…" He shook his head, unable to resist a bitter smile. "A song so sweet each time I hear it played—but nevertheless no more convincing today than it was years ago."

She pressed her now ramrod-straight back against the leather seat and stared out the side window. "Then take me back to Kit's Lodge, please. I have nothing more to say to you."

"Good." He nodded agreeably. "Then I can talk and you can listen."

He turned the SUV onto the highway and pressed his foot on the accelerator. "I've been reading your blog since last November, ever since the city council and chamber of commerce first decided to storm the gates for inclusion."

She continued to gaze out the window, refusing to acknowledge his comment, so he continued. "It's well done. Entertaining. I can see why it's become popular."

Only the blast of the heater fan and the rhythmic squeak of windshield wipers slapping away the lightly falling snow filled the silence that followed his words.

"But…after reviewing years of archived posts, it became clear that the content, the tone, has changed over time. It's become bolder. More provocative. Tackling issues at a deeper level. If that's what it takes to drive more traffic to your site then that's your business. However—"

She whipped toward him, fire in her eyes. "However what?"

How well he remembered that look. That spunk. He'd been drawn to it. Delighted in it. But he'd learned his lesson the hard way.

"This is my home." He spoke with deliberate restraint, recognizing he'd started off all wrong. He'd riled her up too much and now she was ready for a fight. But that wasn't what he wanted. He needed her cooperation, not opposition. "The people you're trying to extract stories from are my friends and neighbors."

"And?"

"They aren't accustomed to dealing with the media. For the most part they're open, transparent and trusting. They don't realize the blog's tasty morsels of thinly veiled gossip and tongue-in-cheek humor might hurt or embarrass them and their loved ones when it's their own personal lives spotlighted on the web."

"So, what are you?" She seasoned her words with an unconvincing sweetness of tone. "The town's official media cop?"

"I'm an elected official." He reached out to cut back the heat. It was sweltering in here now—or was that just him getting hot under the collar? "A city councilman. I represent these people."

He deliberately didn't mention this was also a critical time for his own future. Even though he'd only been on the council a year, he hoped to be appointed to the vice mayor position left vacant last week when Parker Benedict stepped down for health reasons. He stood a chance, but he knew it was a long shot. He didn't need a past shared with Macy Colston interfering with his prospects.

To his annoyance, her sudden lilting laugh unexpectedly warmed his heart, leaving him aching to hear more.

"Well, hello, Mr. Councilman." She tilted her head, eyes now dancing. "You yourself said the city council decided to bring me here. Remember? You chose to compete with hundreds and hundreds of other small towns."

Caught off guard by her captivating smile, he studied her a long moment, their history momentarily forgotten. After all this time here she sat right next to him, every bit as alive and vibrant as he remembered. He had only to reach out and...

He drew a steadying breath, eyes again riveted on the road. "I voted against it."

Of course he had.

Still reeling from the shock of finding Jake in Canyon Springs, Macy stared at his solemn, rugged profile and desperately wished the rest of the council had sided with him. She'd looked forward to this trip, to the opportunity it held for her blog, for her future. But now she wanted to be anywhere except sitting next to him, knowing he still didn't understand her or her dreams. Her goals. He didn't *want* to understand.

He still believed she'd deliberately used both him and his accountant friend who'd told him of questionable practices where his friend worked. Jake's harsh accusations from when she'd run with the story still rang in her ears. Selfish ambition. Unworthy of trust. Betrayal.

She forced herself to maintain what she hoped was a pert smile, one that didn't reveal the pain twisting in her heart. "Nevertheless, your town went all out to get me here with a convincing campaign."

A muscle tightened in his jaw. "I'm aware of that."

"So are you suggesting I let them down? Pack up and move on to the next town on my schedule?"

No doubt that's exactly what he'd like. She could see it clearly written all over him, from the top of his dark brown, sun-streaked hair to the tips of his well-oiled Western boots. Was it the same pair she teased him about the first day they'd met? She brushed the thought away, refusing to get sucked into memories of the past. She could see the resolve to be rid of her in the grim set of his mouth, the rigidity of his broad shoulders and the strong, steady hands clenching the steering wheel.

Half a dozen years had passed, but time had only lent him a stronger aura of unbending determination. Had she, years ago, only wishfully imagined she'd coaxed out a softer, more playful side? Nevertheless, he was still a handsome, appealing man who surprisingly didn't yet sport a wedding band. She kicked herself for noticing.

"I'm only asking," he continued, "that you remember these are real people with real lives. They aren't celebrities striving to catch the world's eye."

"But isn't that why the town competed to have me come here? So the community *can* catch the world's eye?" Her lips twitched in an amusement that belied the tightness in her throat. "Don't think for a moment I'm unaware my blog has become a significant promotional tool for small towns across the country. Everywhere I go puts forgotten little places in the limelight, increasing tourism and drawing business. You think I'm using people to promote my blog, but maybe I'm the one being used."

Jake chuckled, but she sensed he didn't share her perspective. "All I'm asking is that you not exploit anyone for your own purposes. I think you owe me that."

Her breath caught. "Patrick never would have come forward, Jake, and you know it. Not if I hadn't put the story out there."

"You didn't know him like I did. He needed time."

"Time for what? For his colleagues to further misappropriate funds? I waited and waited to see what he'd do. But when he sat on it for weeks…"

"It took Patrick over a year to find another job. Did you know that? No one would trust him enough to hire him after you wrecked his reputation. He could have gone to jail."

A shaft of cold pierced through her, more chilling than the snow she'd stepped through with sandaled feet. "But he didn't."

"No thanks to you."

"I did the right thing."

"Keep telling yourself that, Macy."

She strengthened her grip on the purse in her lap.

"I'm a journalist. What we're called to share with the public doesn't always make us feel great."

"*Called* to share? Or share because it grabs the headlines? Gets picked up by a news wire service and blasted across the country with your byline? Your blog may not be a front-page newspaper story, but it's still read all over the country. All I'm asking, Macy, is out of respect for me and a town I've come to care for that you'll give me your word not to cross any lines."

She didn't expect to unearth any shattering news in this tiny, off-the-beaten-path burg. But in principle, she couldn't promise to willingly suppress anything the public had a legitimate right to know. "Our definitions of what constitutes line-crossing conflict, so please don't ask me to do that."

His firm jaw clenched. "I see."

But he didn't. He never had. If she could go back in time, maybe she'd handle the situation differently. Or maybe she wouldn't. Shady dealings deserved to be exposed. She still believed in the freedom of the press. Still had an instinctive hunger for searching out "the rest of the story" even though she now covered human interest ones rather than the investigative sort. And she still knew that a man who couldn't wholeheartedly support her career choice wasn't the man for her. Hadn't that been what her mother drilled in to her time and time again? Mom should know, if anyone did.

"You're not to tell anyone we knew each other previously," he continued. "Understand?"

Not a request, a demand, reinforcing what he'd already made clear—he didn't want to be associated with her. She could only nod her response, also preferring no one knew she shared a past with this hard-hearted, mulish man.

Jake abruptly slowed the vehicle and swung wide onto the snow-covered, graveled shoulder. For a moment she feared he intended to stop and press his point. But instead, brows lowered, he made a tight U-turn and drove back to town in silence.

Chapter Two

He'd hoped their paths would never cross again.

But gazing down from his Main Street office window to where Macy hurried through the lightly falling snow—coatless, hatless and feet still wedged into those ridiculously citified sandals—he'd clearly hoped in vain.

He stepped slightly back from the window as she glanced up at the two-story, natural stone buildings and then looked around her, almost as if aware of being watched. His chest tightened when she tossed back her hair in a still-familiar gesture, revealing a face every bit as beautiful—and determined—as he remembered.

Heaven help him.

"Look, Jake," a gruff voice interrupted his reverie, "are you listening to anything I've said?"

Jake composed a smile and turned to the balding man who'd barged into his office only minutes ago, Western felt hat in hand. It wouldn't do for the town's mayor to pick up on how the sight of Macy had shaken him. As always when dealing with the perceptive Macon T. "Gus" Gustoffsen, he'd be on his best behavior. You never knew but an endorsement for the vice mayorship—and on down the road one by an outgoing mayor for an incoming one—might be worth biding your time and curtailing your temper.

"I haven't missed a single word."

The sixty-year-old huffed his disbelief. "As I was saying, this is a once-in-a-lifetime opportunity. Macy Colston is due to arrive later today, and I'm depending on you to make sure she gets whatever she needs to put Canyon Springs on the map."

Jake reseated himself behind his grandfather's beloved old desk, disinclined to mention Macy had already arrived a few hours ago, well in advance of the evening's official welcome reception. It was an event Jake wouldn't be attending due to a prior commitment. He nodded to a topographical image of the state of Arizona gracing the wall. "Last time I looked, we've been on the map for eighty-five years, even if not legally incorporated the entire time."

The mayor grimaced as he pulled out a handkerchief and wiped his brow. "You know what I mean. The town's counting on the publicity she generates to lure in fresh faces and cold hard cash. We need to play extra nice and not do anything to get ourselves on her wrong side."

It was a little too late to be concerned with that....

Jake cleared his throat. "As you know, I've got my hands full with more pressing matters. I'm sure Don and Larry can be trusted to handle it. Maybe Hector or Bernie."

Gus stuffed the handkerchief back in his pocket and lowered his towering frame into one of the upholstered leather chairs. Loosening the bolo tie that accented his Western-cut shirt, he shot a cautious look at Jake. "Don't misunderstand me. It's not that I don't trust Don and Larry or either of the others."

"Well, then?"

"It's just that you have a winning way about you, Jake." Gus squinted one eye. "A polish. A gift with words that the others can't hold a candle to. And none of the guys are anything near fancy enough to catch the eye of a pretty city lady."

Jake reached for a ballpoint pen, his thumb rhythmically clicking the retraction mechanism as the striking features of the "pretty city lady" flashed vividly through his memory. But pretty is as pretty does, as his grandmother was known to say.

"It's the town that's in the spotlight here, isn't it? Not one of us."

"That's a fact." Gus nodded vigorously. "But I don't doubt you could talk the moon down out of the sky if you had a mind to. You can win her over on our behalf, make sure she does the town justice."

Jake shook his head. "I'm afraid you'll have to find someone else."

Gus scowled. "You've been a promoter of this

town since you moved here half a dozen years ago, but you were the lone dissenting vote against participating in the competition. I still don't understand what you have against the idea when you know how it will help our town."

"It's not that I—" How could he explain it without divulging matters he'd rather not divulge? Rolling back from the desk, he took pleasure in the comforting creak of the old-fashioned wooden chair. It was a perfect match to the desk that dignified his book-lined office, but he'd paid a steep price for it, figuratively if not literally.

Gus smacked his beefy hand on the desktop enthusiastically, mistakenly interpreting Jake's sudden silence as evidence that he was making persuasive inroads. "Her blog is nearly as popular as that rancher woman's. You know, the gal who also has the food show? My wife says she almost feels as if she knows her, and that's how Macy comes across, too. Like you could sit down next to her for a long, cozy chat."

Jake managed not to choke. Sit down for a chat? Right. That's exactly how she wanted people to feel—it's how she got them to lower their guard and open up to her.

He straightened, his gaze lingering on the framed photo of his grandparents, the only decorative item on his desk. "Look, I think Larry and Don or one of the others will do fine. She seems to take a fancy to local color. You can't beat them for that."

"No, but…" Gus darted a guarded look in his

direction. "Larry, Don and Hector are married. Macy's not."

Jake chuckled. "Do you think Andrea, Melissa and Dionne won't let their men out of their sight as long as Ms. Colston's in town?"

"Not exactly." The big man fiddled with his wristwatch. Gus might look and speak like a country boy at times, but he was a shrewd businessman. Something was on his mind even though he was taking his sweet time getting around to it. "You're not married, Jake."

Jake placed the pen on his desk and pinned the mayor with a frank look. "Where are you going with this?"

Gus reached again for the handkerchief and mopped his forehead. "Married men have obligations. Commitments. Loyalties. They have to be careful not to give anyone the wrong impression."

"And?"

Gus wadded the handkerchief in his fist. "As a single man, you're a free agent, so to speak. You're at liberty to sweet-talk Macy Colston into portraying us in the most favorable light without anyone questioning your behavior."

"What exactly do you mean by *sweet-talk?*"

Gus glanced at the snow dancing outside the window rather than meeting Jake's gaze. "You know… turn on the charm. Sweep her off her feet. Put stars in her eyes."

Jake stared at the now-blushing mayor. "Are you

saying you want me to fake a romantic interest in this journalist to manipulate her impressions of Canyon Springs?"

"Who's to say you'd have to fake it?" Gus's expression brightened. "She's more than pretty. Smart, too. You're a good-lookin' man, or so my wife and oldest daughter tell me. On the sober side, maybe. But you're easy enough to get along with most of the time, just like your grandfather was. With some effort on your part, I bet you and Macy would hit it off."

No way would he woo Macy Colston, no matter how noble the cause. He'd steer clear of her in the coming weeks, keeping an eye on her through her blog posts and stepping in only if a questionable situation warranted it. Even if he had any interest in seeing more of the woman—which he didn't—he had more pressing obligations than babysitting a tenacious journalist. Seeing to Grandma's welfare for one. The Canyon Springs history book for another. And he had to make sure the city council didn't do something stupid with the property his grandfather had willed to the town. What had Granddad been thinking when he'd done that anyway?

"Now look, Gus, you know I don't—"

The big man waved him away. "If you want to get the rest of the council on your side about what to do with that prime bit of real estate the city inherited, it might serve you well to put effort into this. You know, prove you're a team player."

Gus had a point. Even though he didn't vocalize

Jake's added hopes for the vice mayorship, Jake knew the other man was thinking about it, too. There were those who still said his election last year was a fluke considering his sole opposition had abruptly withdrawn from the race. But then again, this was Macy they were talking about....

"Can't spare the time, Gus."

"You work too hard. Need to loosen up." The older man folded his arms. "If you won't step up for the good of the town, do it for yourself. Have a little fun for a change. This might be your last chance to catch the eye of a looker like Macy Colston. You're—what? Thirty-two? Thirty-three?"

Thirty-five.

"Give it a shot, Councilman. What do you have to lose?"

Jake stood and punched the intercom button on his desk phone. "Phyllis Diane, would you please call Rob McGuire? I'm supposed to meet him at Singing Rock. Tell him I'm on my way and I apologize in advance for being a few minutes late."

"Happy to oblige, Jake," his office assistant responded with a soft Texas drawl. Always amiable, even when putting in Saturday overtime hours, he nevertheless figured it was only a matter of time before she headed for greener pastures and left him and his law partner high and dry.

He pressed the off button and, mustering a smile, snagged his Windbreaker from the antique coat tree behind him. "I appreciate your confidence in my persuasive abilities, Mr. Mayor, but this case is officially closed."

Macy's cell phone played a merry tune and she crossed the room to pull it from the purse she'd left on what looked to be a homemade quilted bedspread. In fact, everything she'd seen of this two-story log cabin lodge and restaurant oozed rustic charm, from its wooden-planked porch to a natural stone fireplace in the lobby to her antiques-filled room. The whole town held such promise…if it wasn't for Jake calling Canyon Springs home.

"It's about time you answered." The familiar voice of her agent-publicist carried across the miles with her usual crisp, no-nonsense tone. You'd have thought she was a native New Yorker and not a Midwestern transplant.

"Hey, sis." Brushing back her hair, Macy sat on the bed and kicked off her sandals. She'd have to buy more substantial footwear for the coming days if this weather kept up. A heavier coat, too. Maybe gloves.

"So are you at your next assignment yet?"

"I checked in right before lunch. But I should have brought boots."

"It's raining?"

"Snowing."

Silence. Then came a cautious query. "The schedule shows you're in Arizona…right?"

Macy envisioned her older sister, brow puckered as she shook back her pricey, chin-length bob.

"Nicole, do you remember how we were told Canyon Springs would give my readers a different perspective on the Grand Canyon state? Well, they weren't kidding. It's smack in the middle of a huge forest of ponderosa pines. Flocked in white at the moment. Absolutely breathtaking."

"But it's April."

"And it looks like Christmas." She returned to the window, where fluffy flakes still descended lightly. "I plan to get out and snap a few more photos. With temperatures spiking over much of the country, my readers will love this."

"Which reminds me of why I called you. I heard from Vanessa this morning."

Vanessa Riker was the contact person for Macy's primary blog sponsor, a rapidly expanding chain of organic food store-restaurant combos.

"She mentioned," Nicole continued, "that their new board is coming close to a decision on increasing their sponsorship. You know what that means, don't you?"

Macy's spirits rose in anticipation. "It means I'm closer to doing this full time. No more scrimping to get by. No more cramming in freelance work on the side."

"It's bigger than that. Vanessa says they're not only discussing covering publication costs of a book, but a series of books gleaned from your blog posts. You'd retain the rights, but they'd be exclusively available at all their locations and on their website—with a sweeter than sweet royalty deal for you. And—"

Macy drew in a breath. There was an *and?*

"—Vanessa said they see real marketing potential tied to your blog. In fact, they asked me to see if you'd be interested in doing a television program."

At her sister's words, Macy lowered herself onto an oak rocking chair. She'd hoped for something like this, but hadn't expected to see it happen so soon. "A television show?"

"They've contacted an independent agency to see about the possibility of creating and pitching a pilot to a specialty network. She mentioned there's genuine interest on their part in committing to commercial time for such a program."

"Wow."

"It's still in the brainstorming stage, but something along the lines of a reality-type program. You know, traveling across America to visit little towns just like you do now. But Vanessa mentioned that in order to justify an investment of that magnitude, you need higher numbers on your blog to draw more traffic to their business. And to get that, you need to give your readers more of what's being asked for."

Something juicy. Uncovering a local scandal piece by piece, with cliffhangers from blog to blog. Something Jake would certainly be dead set against, but she wasn't about to mention to her sister his presence or his opposition. Like Mom, she'd remember Jake from Macy's university days. They already believed he'd derailed her from a promising career in investigative journalism, undermining her confidence in the direction she'd been heading.

Stop chasing butterflies, her mother had frequently warned her when as a child she'd failed to apply herself to a task at hand. She'd done well to follow that admonition—until Jake came along and she'd nearly allowed herself to get sidetracked. But she was back in the saddle and galloping toward a goal once more. Her professional blogging and human interest story freelancing hadn't won any accolades from her family—until now—and she wasn't about to be unseated again.

"It never ceases to amaze me," Nicole continued, "how transparent people are willing to be with you in exchange for their fifteen minutes of fame."

Macy laughed. "I'd be surprised, too, if there isn't a juicy story hidden in the closet of every little town."

At least that was her hope.

"Vanessa says while they've seen gradual improvement with the direction you've taken lately, you can't rely on lame revelations like that recent one about the youth group leader. You know, the one who slipped a bucket of Dairy Queen into his hand-crank ice cream maker and passed it off as his own at a church social."

"You have to admit it was funny." Macy smiled, remembering. "He good-naturedly admitted his deception once people started asking him for the recipe."

Nicole scoffed. "That might be fine for a blog, Macy. All warm and fuzzy. But for TV? Major yawner. Once a sponsor of this caliber promises to invest in you at a level they're intending, you have to deliver what they want."

"The board needs to remember it's the everyday-ness of the blog that draws people." Rising from the rocker, Macy again returned to the window. "It's a peek into small-town life. The hopes, dreams, challenges and rewards of living outside the fast lane. It's a lifestyle that seems, from the popularity of the blog, to be one that a big chunk of America wishes they could slow down enough to join in on."

Nicole laughed. "Listen to yourself, Macy. It sounds as if you're buying into your own spin and have forgotten this blog is merely the means to an end."

"I haven't forgotten." She traced a finger along the window's polished wooden frame. "I don't want a sponsor sucking the heart out of it, that's all. People have certain expectations and those will carry over to a TV program, too."

"I'm just saying—" Nicole's voice took on an impatient edge "—if you're content to do a low-key, chatty little blog for the rest of your life, that's your choice. But I thought you enlisted my help because you wanted to make something of this. Something big."

And take her sister along for the increasingly lucrative ride?

She often felt guilty that her highly successful sister spent valuable time on *Hometowns With Heart* negotiations with relatively little recompense thus far.

"I still want that." She drew a strengthening breath, hope rising at the possibilities almost within reach. Surely she could ramp up the blog to make it more exciting and still stay in control of the voice and tone she wanted to protect. Nicole just wanted what was best for all of them. "I couldn't have gotten this far without your help. And Mom's, of course. It's just that…well, everything is happening so fast."

"We've got to strike while the iron is hot. Chances like this can evaporate in the blink of an eye. Are you still on board?"

For a fleeting moment she recalled the set of Jake's jaw and the flatness of his expression when she'd told him she could make no promises. Her mother was right about so many things. Surely she was right that Macy was better off without the influence of a man like that in her life.

"Yes, of course. I'm completely on board."

Chapter Three

"At least she didn't say anything about me in her first post from Canyon Springs, Abe." Jake stared at the laptop he'd placed on the kitchen table next to his Sunday morning breakfast. "As an elected official, I sure don't want to get a reputation as being an opponent of the press. That could haunt me to the steps of the state capitol. I'll have to be more careful around her. Stay on my toes. Or better yet, avoid her altogether."

He scrolled through the *Hometowns With Heart* blog again, studying several photos taken of the snowy landscape outside Kit's Lodge. It was quite a contrast from the saguaro cactus and bright flowers she'd posted the previous morning from Phoenix— the Valley of the Sun. His gaze lingered on one photo in particular.

"There she is, buddy, in her sandals and sundress next to a scrawny, two-foot high snowman. Can you believe it?"

He shook his head and glanced over at Abe, who sat patiently by the back door, his brown beagle eyes trained hopefully on his master. Jake smiled. He loved that dog even though it had been Macy who'd badgered him into adopting the little guy from the Central Missouri Humane Society. A puppy, of all things, which had to be potty trained, then fed and walked every day. He'd never done anything that crazy in his whole life. But then, his brain had come unglued during those seven or eight months he'd spent around Macy.

It wasn't a period in his life he was proud of.

And yet…

Abe—named after Jake's favorite president— whimpered.

"Hang on, I'm almost done here." He took another bite of oatmeal, his attention once again trained on the graceful form and laughing eyes of the pretty journalist. She seemed to be enjoying herself, oblivious to the whipping wind that had blown her long hair into a golden aura.

Mouth suddenly dry, Jake drank the remainder of his orange juice. He knew now he'd fallen for her, a woman like none he'd ever met, that first day at the estate sale. Most women considered him too stodgy. Staid. Too focused on the needs of his clients. It's what made him a good attorney. But he hadn't had the experience—or the sense—to recognize his own vulnerability to a flirtatious female who acted as if he was the most tempting thing she'd ever seen on her love life's menu.

Last fall he hadn't felt compelled to enlighten his fellow council members on the history he shared with the vivacious blogger...and risk losing their hard-earned respect. Keeping silent hadn't seemed too chancy. After all, what were the statistical odds of his hometown being selected from among hundreds vying for her attention?

Pretty high as it turned out.

"I feel as if I should warn everyone, Abe, but wouldn't sharing now what I know of her be akin to closing the barn door after the horse got out?"

And how would his clients and constituency react? Would they be able to trust a man who'd broken a professional confidence all because he'd let his guard down with a woman who wasn't even his wife? He could almost hear the snickers, the comparison of his indiscretion to that of the biblical Sampson and Delilah. That wasn't something he needed with the vice mayor opening up for grabs.

The tricolored dog whined, almost as if recognizing what Jake knew too well. That, regrettably, his earlier decision to withhold the whole story could end up a sin of omission he and the entire town might come to regret.

"Okay, maybe I came on too strong with her yesterday. Gus is right, none of us need to be getting ourselves on her wrong side." He scrolled down through the blog post again, then back to the photo. "Do you think I should apologize?"

Abe moved restlessly by the door just as Jake caught a glimpse of the clock above the sink. "Whoa!"

He looked down in alarm at his grungy sweats, then jumped to his feet and rapidly crossed the floor. Opening the door to the fenced-in backyard, he motioned to Abe. "You'd better get out there and do your business, mister, or I'll be late for church."

Would Macy be there? Would he have an opportunity to talk to her and smooth things over? Could he prevent a well-meaning churchgoer from signing her up for the prayer chain calls? That privilege would provide her with direct access to every illness, financial problem, kid woe or faltering marriage in town.

He'd better get moving.

As it turned out, he needn't have rushed. Even with a slight detour to pass by the property Granddad had willed to the city, something that had become a habit in recent days to assure himself all was still as it should be, he was among the early arrivals for the worship service at Canyon Springs Christian Church.

"How's the book going?" The youthful-looking pastor, Jason Kenton, handed him a stack of bulletins for distribution. As a deacon, one of Jake's many church-related responsibilities was to meet and greet on Sunday mornings.

"It's coming along." Although not nearly as fast as he'd hoped. He wished Grandma had mentioned months ago that Granddad was working on a history of the town, hoping to have it printed for the community's eighty-fifth birthday celebration at the end of next month. Jake was determined to finish it.

Surprisingly, or maybe not so surprisingly considering how Granddad was never one to brag about himself, he hadn't included a chapter on his own life as one of the town's influential citizens. Jake intended to rectify that omission. But the clock was ticking.

"Lots of people are looking forward to reading that book." The pastor scrubbed his hand along his close-cropped beard. "Hey, I guess you already know the *Hometowns With Heart* lady arrived yesterday. Reyna and the kids met her at a welcome reception at Kit's last night. I'd stayed here late to polish up my sermon notes, so I missed out."

"She'll be here for a month. I'm sure you'll get your opportunity." *But don't say anything to her you don't want to see in her blog.* Jake held up the bulletins, not eager to continue a conversation about Macy. "I'd better get to my post."

He tucked his Bible under his arm and stationed himself on the sidewalk between the parking lot and main entrance to the native-stone building set back in the pines. The air was pleasantly cool and pine scented but, typical of springtime snows, yesterday's frosty deposit had all but melted away. Only traces remained in the most deeply shaded areas.

Jake raised his hand in greeting at the approaching Diaz family, a pang of envy reverberating as he watched second-grader Davy proudly grasp the hand of his father and that of his very pregnant stepmother. Joe had announced at the church's Thanksgiving feast last fall that he and his wife, high school teacher Meg, had a baby conveniently timed to arrive when the spring semester concluded.

"Good to see you, Joe." Jake shook his friend's hand. "You, too, Meg."

The perky brunette rolled her eyes. "There's a lot more of me to see than there used to be."

Jake grinned and ruffled Davy's hair, then watched thoughtfully as the family entered the building. Father and son bonds—that's something he didn't know much about firsthand from either the father or son standpoint.

"Jake!"

He turned to see Paris Perslow approaching from the education wing. A dark-haired young woman with smoke-gray eyes, Paris was the epitome of class. Elegance.

This morning she was dressed in a cranberry wool jacket, matching skirt and black heels, reminding him why in recent days he'd given serious consideration to asking her out. She'd make a perfect partner for a man in public office. Active in social and charitable organizations, she had an impeccable reputation. They had much in common, too, as descendants of the town's most respected residents. Most important, he couldn't imagine her ever betraying a trust. Only the fact that a sadness still lingered in her eyes from the death of her fiancé several years ago had held him back.

But maybe it was time to help her—and himself—move on?

"Good morning, Paris."

She smiled that gracious smile of hers, but before he could tell her how lovely she looked, something behind him caught her attention. With a soft gasp of delight, her delicate eyebrows lifted. "That's *her,* isn't it?"

Her?

He followed Paris's riveted gaze toward the parking lot. Don James, fellow councilman and brother of Larry, had arrived with his family and he was holding open the vehicle's door for none other than Macy Colston. Wearing a trim, belted, turquoise dress, a white sweater draped over her shoulders, she glowed with eagerness as her gaze swept her surroundings.

He should have known Macy wouldn't miss church. While she hadn't grown up in a believing family and had had her share of faith struggles, by the time he'd met her as a senior in college she'd made that life-changing decision.

"It *is* the *Hometowns with Heart* woman." Paris moved forward, excitement now lighting her eyes. "Did you see her blog this morning with the adorable snowman? Come on, Jake, let's go meet her."

When he held back, she turned, her gaze questioning. Then she laughed. "You've already met her haven't you? I forgot as a city councilman you have a front row seat to welcome incoming celebrities."

Like Canyon Springs got many of those.

"Yeah, I've met her." Over Paris's shoulder he could see Macy heading toward the church, Don's two grade school-aged grandchildren hopping along beside her and chatting excitedly. They wouldn't be readers of her blog, but apparently someone had conveyed that she wasn't your average church service visitor.

Behind Macy's back, a curly-haired Don grinned at him like a kid who'd been let in on a big secret. He nodded knowingly toward the pretty blonde, signaling with a thumbs-up.

Jake frowned.

"Oh, don't be grumpy." Paris, having missed Don's antics behind her, grasped his arm and tugged gently. "Introduce me properly so she doesn't think I'm only another rabid fan."

He needed to speak to Macy in private, not in a superficial social setting with Don clowning around in the background. But gazing into Paris's hope-filled eyes, what other choice did he have?

The moment she stepped from the SUV, Macy spotted Jake with the stylishly dressed woman and her heart inexplicably lurched. No, he didn't wear a ring, but her hasty conclusion that there was no one special in his life was obviously erroneous.

Now they approached her as a couple, the smiling woman's arm linked with Jake's. With the older councilman's rambunctious grandkids hanging on to her own hands, she felt at a disadvantage as the stunning female closed the ground between them.

Jake appeared uncomfortable as well, although whether from remembering how their last encounter had ended in Kit's parking lot yesterday or because he'd neglected to mention a lady in his life, she couldn't be sure. While the omission irritated her, she couldn't hold it against him since she hadn't commented on her own relationship status. Besides, other topics had dominated their heated discussion.

Thankfully, Don's wife stepped forward to pry the hands of her granddaughters from Macy's, then herded the girls toward the church.

"Good morning, Macy." Jake, looking more handsome today than yesterday, nodded a greeting. "I'd like you to meet Paris Perslow. Paris, this is Macy Colston, of *Hometowns With Heart* fame."

The woman released Jake's arm and reached out exquisitely manicured hands to grasp Macy's. "I know you've probably heard this a million times, but your blog almost makes me feel as if I know you, Macy."

This sophisticated-looking woman read her blog? That must annoy Jake to no end considering he'd voted against bringing its host here. Had he told her about their regrettable past relationship? If she had an awareness of shared history between her man and

Macy, Paris's serene expression didn't reveal any tell-tale signs.

"It's always wonderful to be welcomed like an old friend wherever I go." Macy avoided Jake's gaze, concerned his lady friend might pick up on it if she gave him a too-pointed stare. "That's one of the joys of my blog."

"I can't believe you're here in Canyon Springs. I've been reading your posts for years." Paris smiled up at Jake. "Remember that rhubarb cobbler you couldn't get enough of at the Labor Day picnic last year? It's a recipe Macy shared from a quaint Ozark restaurant."

Labor Day. So they'd been together for a while. Macy forced a smile. "I loved that place. It had the best barbecue I think I've ever tasted."

"It was back in the trees along a creek, wasn't it? A feisty black gal who'd once been a New York City chef ran it."

Macy laughed. "You remember all that?"

"I'm a faithful reader." Paris leaned in as if confiding in an old acquaintance. "Probably half the town is. Even more, I'm sure, once it was announced you were coming."

"Ladies." Jake tapped the face of his watch. "It's nearing time for the worship service to start and I still have a handful of these."

He lifted a stack of church bulletins.

Still smiling, Paris patted his arm. "Then why don't you run on ahead and take care of business. We'll join you later."

From the mildly surprised look on his face, he wasn't too keen on leaving them together. But with an indulgent nod of her head, Paris gave him a gentle shove and sent him on his way.

"Now you have to tell me," she continued with a wink, "how things turned out for that Colorado couple last month. I felt there had to be more to the story...."

To Macy's delight, Paris wasn't the only one who greeted her with the warmth of a long-lost family member. At the potluck in the fellowship hall following the service—given in her honor, no less—numerous ladies invited her to share a meal, probably hoping one of their old family recipes would be featured in the blog. Some hugged her. One elderly lady—Mae Harding, was it?—kissed her cheek as she might do to her granddaughter.

Sharon Dixon, owner of Dix's Woodland Warehouse, confirmed Macy's work schedule at the general store on Main Street. As was her custom when visiting small communities, she often served in an unpaid capacity at local businesses, finding it gave her a better opportunity to get to know those who populated the town.

Others crowded in to introduce themselves and their families. Some handed her business cards—numerous campgrounds, cabin resorts and RV parks. An outdoorsy crowd, it seemed.

Macy smiled, listened and asked questions, mentally tabulating how she'd portray the flavor of the town in her blog. But her greatest "find" in the lunchtime crowd was when three sets of newlyweds eagerly shared their stories of recent Christmastime nuptials. Her *Hometowns With Heart* online friends loved it when she covered true-life romance.

Speaking of which…she'd lost track of Jake and Paris some time ago.

With councilmen Don and Larry and their spouses drifting to a dessert-laden table, she stepped away from the corner where they'd had her pinned and scanned the room. Oh. There *she* was at least, across the room chatting with the pastor's wife. Macy knew she herself wasn't any slouch when it came to mingling in social situations, but nevertheless envy stabbed as she watched Paris's poised interaction. As much as she hated to admit it, she'd be a good match for Jake in his role as a public servant. Did his dreams still extend beyond his current council seat?

"Macy?"

The familiar masculine voice and light touch to her upper arm startled her. She turned, heart skittering expectantly.

"I'm sorry to tear you away from your fans," Jake said, keeping his voice low, "but there's someone I think you should meet."

Jake helping her? After yesterday, she was surprised he was speaking to her at all.

"Or actually two someones," he added, "you might want to feature in your blog."

Detecting an unmistakable glimmer of amusement

in his eyes, she folded her arms and gave him a suspicious glare.

His lips twitched, but he managed to suppress the smile. "Come and see."

She glanced around, but since no one appeared to be waiting to speak with her—and Jake's lady friend seemed otherwise occupied—she nodded, her curiosity piqued.

He led the way outside to the back of the property. Pine trees overshadowed a scattering of picnic tables and a concrete slab boasted a basketball hoop, neither of which seemed newsworthy. She slowed her pace. Had Jake lured her out here to give her another piece of his mind?

He disappeared around the side of the building as her sandaled feet picked a path across the thick carpet of still-damp, brown pine needles. But just when she'd convinced herself to go back inside, the sound of a horse nickering close by reached her ears.

A horse? At the church?

That's all it took to send her around the corner in Jake's wake. Yes, a horse. Two, in fact, saddled and tied to a hitching post. Bridles removed and draped over saddle horns, each horse had been secured with a lead rope fastened to its halter. One of them leaned his head into Jake, eager to have a sweet spot behind his ear scratched.

"People ride horses to church here?" Talk about the Wild West. She approached slowly, not wanting to spook the animals. They were beautiful, with intelligent, gentle brown eyes.

"The pastor's brother, Trey Kenton, and Trey's wife, Kara, do when the weather's suitable. Meet Beamer and Taco."

Kara and Trey. That would be the woman with the strawberry-blond ponytail and the soft-spoken cowboy with a slight limp. They were one of the December wedding couples. What an ideal addition to tomorrow's blog this would make. A true taste of high country Arizona that would appeal to her readers. Perfect.

"I'll get them from inside, along with my camera." She spun away.

"Macy. Wait."

At the sharp command, she halted and hesitantly turned toward him. "I want to see if they'll come out and pose for me."

"I'm sure they'd be happy to. But they aren't going anywhere just yet. I saw Trey cutting himself a whopping big piece of cherry pie as we were leaving." He cracked a smile. "So, pardon the expression, but hold your horses."

Macy's throat constricted. Despite the pun, she read something else in his now unsmiling blue eyes. Something she wasn't in any mood to deal with right now.

"Look, Jake—"

Chapter Four

Nostrils flaring, the chestnut Taco suddenly lifted his head and emitted a powerfully shrill whinny that startled Macy into silence.

Having detected the preemptive strike intention in Macy's tone, Jake laughed and gave his equine friend a grateful pat. Perfect timing. He had something he wanted to say and the challenge he sensed in her words would have put him on the defensive. "I think you'd better get over here, Mace, and give these guys some attention. I don't remember you being afraid of horses."

"I'm not."

He sensed her indecision, though. Should she allow herself to be distracted or pick up where she'd left off? She again approached, probably more uneasy around him at the moment than she was the tethered horses.

Beamer stretched his neck toward her and she patted the top of his nose. He pushed forward to sniff her and she quickly stepped back to prevent him from getting anything on that pretty dress.

"Here. I snagged these off a veggie tray." Jake fished in his jacket pocket and handed her a carrot stick. "Place it on the flat of your hand at the base of your fingers. Keep your fingers together and thumb tucked to the side. Then arch your hand downward and let him lip it off."

"He won't bite me?"

"Naw." He pulled out another carrot stick and demonstrated with Taco. Beamer pushed in, looking for his fair share, and Jake nodded to Macy. "Go ahead. He's ready for his."

Gingerly, she held out her hand as Jake had instructed and immediately Beamer's lips grazed her palm, searching for the treat. Finding it, he slipped it into his mouth and stepped back to crunch it. Loudly.

Macy laughed. "He didn't waste any time."

Jake handed her another carrot, but from her cautious glance in his direction she seemed to sense he was biding his time. And he was. After the passage of time, you'd think he'd have had anything he intended to say engraved in his memory, but having her here, right now, his mind drew a blank.

She toyed with the carrot in her hand. "You know, Jake, this is going to be a long four weeks for both of us if you intend to monitor my comings and goings each and every day."

"I always go to church. Ask anybody."

"Nevertheless, considering yesterday's conversation, don't tell me it hasn't crossed your mind to keep an eye on me."

A corner of his mouth turned up in admission. He patted Taco's neck, then again scratched behind the big animal's ear. "I wanted to talk to you about that."

"That's what I thought." Her voice held a note of resignation.

He kept his eyes trained on the horse now rummaging for another treat. "I want to apologize for yesterday, Macy."

From the intake of her breath, that was the last thing she expected to hear come out of his mouth. Studying her thoughtfully, he gently pushed the horse's head away. "We had ourselves a little standoff, didn't we?"

Her words came softly. "I'm not the enemy, Jake."

"I know that."

"Well…" She drew another breath. "Yesterday it sure didn't feel like you did."

"I'm sorry."

If the sudden crease on her smooth forehead was any indication, she wasn't convinced of his sincerity. Maybe a contrite Jake wasn't something she'd been accustomed to in the past?

"People all over the country love my blog." She motioned to the building next to them. "As you saw, towns love my slant on their communities and welcome me wherever I go."

Macy slipped another carrot into Beamer's mouth. "You said you've read my posts and admitted they're done well. Why can't you trust me to fairly report my experiences here?"

He glanced at the ground, again avoiding her gaze. "I think we already touched on that."

"I never meant to hurt you or your friend, Jake. You have to believe me."

He met her steady gaze with a questioning one of his own. "That might get you off the hook, but will it make me feel any better about having trusted you with information shared in confidence? Information I knew only because someone trusted *me?*"

"You didn't tell me it was confidential."

His throat tightened. Did she have no idea how he'd felt about her back then? How close he'd come to asking her to become a permanent part of his life? "I shouldn't have had to tell you. That's the thing."

She still didn't get it.

"I was supposed to be a mind reader?"

"I shouldn't have had to preface my every word to my girlfriend with 'not for publication, please.'"

Her eyes widened slightly. "I'm…sorry you feel that way, Jake. I don't know what else to say."

Head bowed as if in defeat, she turned away.

"Macy—"

She didn't look at him.

He kept his voice low, beseeching. "My point is—"

"I think you've made your point, Jake." She raised her head and started toward the church. Then, her back still to him, she abruptly stopped. "Thanks for introducing me to Taco and Beamer."

Shaking back her hair, she briskly rounded the corner of the building.

He could easily have caught up with her before she reached the door, but he didn't follow. For someone who was degreed in dispute resolution, he sure was making a muddle of it with Macy. What he'd intended as a few words to smooth things over ended up in another quarrel that didn't resolve anything.

Maybe he needed to face it. The problems between them would never be resolved. Not as long as he was who he was and she was who she was.

His girlfriend? Is that how Jake had thought of her back then?

Macy stared out the window of the Canyon Springs Historical Museum late Monday afternoon, lost in thought.

Jake had never introduced her as his girlfriend. Never told her he loved her. Never talked about their future except maybe in the vaguest of ways—just enough to feed her dream that she'd found Mr. Right. She'd known she was young, six or seven years his junior and still a student while he'd been out in the real world practicing law for several years. She'd been painfully aware that he might not consider her a permanent fixture in his life. Yet she'd talked herself into being content with the unspoken promises made in the way he'd kissed her....

Macy stepped away from the window, shoving the still-vivid memories of his gentle touch to the far corners of her mind. Things seemed promising at first. But as winter departed and graduation loomed on the horizon, he'd offered no words of hope.

That's when she'd faced reality. Sure, she could at any time have said "put up or shut up." She could have told him to either admit he had feelings for her or keep his kisses to himself. But she hadn't. What woman wanted to whine and bully a man into making her his wife? Although it might have made an amusing story to tell the grandkids.

But had his failure to make a commitment played a part in her decision to run with a news story inspired by his foot-dragging friend? Had Jake's ambiguous behavior provoked her into calling her mother, who had contacts on the company's board and who could stir up an internal investigation?

Of course not. She'd been over this a million times. A story was a story and she'd objectively determined this was one that needed to be told. That was all there was to it. Right?

"If you don't mind, Macy—" Sandi Bradshaw Harding, president of the historical society and one of the three local brides who'd taken marital vows last December, reentered the room. Dark blue eyes apologetic, she tucked a strand of blond, blunt-cut hair behind her ear. "I need to pick up my daughter from her gymnastics lesson. You can continue sorting the photos if you'd like. I shouldn't be gone long."

Sandi checked something off in a red spiral notebook that seemed to keep her—and everyone around her—organized. A high school English teacher, she'd met with Macy after class dismissed for the day to give her the grand tour of the museum. This time of year it was only open on Saturdays or for prearranged visits by school groups and other visitors. But the summer season would start soon, so there was much to be done to get things in order.

For the past hour, Macy had assisted in sorting old photos while Sandi filled her in on her courtship and history of the museum.

When Sandi departed, Macy took the opportunity to further inspect her surroundings, pausing at the photos of Sandi's first husband, Corporal Keith Anderson Bradshaw, who'd died in active duty in the Middle East. Then she moved back to the main room to study the plethora of Canyon Springs mementos from the past, many of them lining the museum's walls. Old photos. Advertisements from the earliest of the town's businesses. Framed maps and newspaper clippings.

Cell phone in hand, she speed-dialed her part-time assistant in St. Louis.

"Ava, I'm so happy you're back from vacation. I have a project for you." She continued to stroll along the perimeters of the room as she pictured her widowed friend. A sharp dresser with an even sharper mind, the African-American woman and Macy were neighbors in a high-rise complex. It had been a moment of mutual good fortune when they'd taken the same elevator up to the twelfth floor three years ago.

They'd immediately become fast friends, and Macy had depended on her ever since to do the necessary research to add historical flavor to the blog.

"I was hoping to hear from you." Ava's soft voice held the barest of St. Louis accents. "Things are slow around here."

Macy doubted that. Ava Darrington probably hadn't had a slow moment since she'd made her debut into the world seven decades ago. Then, following her husband's death, the petite retired college history professor became addicted to genealogy to fill in empty hours and stayed more than busy tracking connections for friends and family.

"Then I'm in luck. I need background on historically prominent townspeople. You know, fun facts."

"You'd mentioned you were heading to a mountain town in Arizona this month."

"Right. I'm working part-time at the Canyon Springs historical museum, so I'm gathering a few names that look promising for further research."

"Let's hear 'em, sweetie."

Macy leaned closer to a grainy photo of a rather tough-looking couple standing by a log cabin, which boasted a hand-written sign proclaiming it as a dry goods store. She read the fine print aloud. "'Orian Bigelow and his wife, Harva.'" She spelled the names. "The photo's caption says circa 1928 and that they were proprietors of the first store and place of lodging in what later became Canyon Springs.

Their story might make interesting reading if you can find any details."

"1928," Ava mused aloud. "So they got their start right before the Great Depression. I'll check it out."

Another photo caught her eye, a group shot featured in a yellowed newspaper clipping. "These next three are scholarship donors to the local school district. Photo 1960. Francine Drew, high school principal. Brewster Mose, physician. Dexter Canton Smith—"

Ava let out a groan. "Oh, please, not another Smith."

Macy laughed as she quickly scanned the article, remembering the hoops Ava had jumped through last year on another man with that last name. "Sorry, but from the sound of the clipping he appears to be a moneyed sort. Maybe he won't be as hard to track as the other one."

Ava sighed. "I'll give it my best shot. Anyone else?"

Macy moved on to a few more photos, studying the captions for backgrounds that might prove interesting to her readers. "The cool thing about Arizona is that since it didn't become a state until 1912, its early years look to be a fascinating blend of old time West and growing modernization."

Macy's gaze lingered longingly on other vintage photos displayed across the wall. Sometimes she wished her role was switched with Ava's. That she'd have time to do the research and Ava would do the blogging.

"So is that it?" Ava sounded eager to get started.

"All for now, thank you. I really appreciate the historical tidbits you unearth." The sound of heavy steps on the porch and the rattle of the door caught her attention. "Sorry, Ava. Gotta run. I think I have my first customer."

She slid the slim phone into a skirt pocket and turned with a welcoming smile just as Jake Talford stepped into the room.

What was *she* doing here?

Jake halted, hand still on the doorknob as he took in Macy's denim skirt, white crinkled blouse—and those strappy sandals. He didn't overlook the frown aimed in his direction either.

With Grandma's visit to Phoenix lingering well into spring, he didn't want to interrupt her with questions about Granddad's past. So it seemed logical to start finding answers in the same place where he intended to verify the research on the other old-time residents featured in Granddad's book. The historical museum.

For a flashing moment he considered returning later, but he and Macy may as well get used to bumping into each other around town for the next month.

He released the doorknob and stepped farther into the room. Then he shut the door to block the coolish wind swirling in around him.

"Good afternoon, Macy."

She lifted her chin, assessing him. "I thought we agreed you weren't going to shadow me."

"We did?" He said that to get a rise out of her and was rewarded by a steely spark in her green eyes. "Actually, I saw a car outside and assumed the museum was open for business. How would I know you'd be here this afternoon?"

She folded her arms. "You could have picked up my schedule from the chamber of commerce."

"I didn't." But he would.

"I won't debate the validity of that denial." Skepticism colored her tone. "But we need to come to an understanding."

"We attempted that twice, didn't we?" He managed a placating smile as he stuffed his hands into his jacket pockets and strolled casually to look at a framed newspaper clipping on the wall. Then he turned to her. "I didn't get a sense you intended to negotiate."

"You didn't want to negotiate, just lay ground rules. Your rules."

"My town." He shrugged and tucked his lips into a "too bad" expression.

"My blog." Her smile mimicked his.

Then, in a dismissive movement, she seated herself at a nearby oak table covered with shallow stacks of old photographs. She picked one up and studied it intently as though he was no longer in the room. Recognizing another face-off in the making, he shifted gears. Thankfully, he hadn't been a topic of conversation in her blog post this morning. Beamer and Taco had won out. But there was no point in pushing his luck.

He peeked into one of the side rooms. "Is Sandi around?"

He should have asked that question first instead of risking being overheard in personal conversation with Macy.

"We're the only ones here, Jake." As if reading his mind, an amused smile touched her lips. She placed the photograph in one of the stacks and reached for another. "She'll be back shortly, after she picks up her daughter."

Should he wait? He'd left work early in hopes the longtime historical society enthusiast could direct him to where Granddad might have gotten his manuscript's facts. Had he done his research here or from the local newspaper's archives or personal interviews? It wasn't that he didn't trust his grandfather's work, but the deeply ingrained legal watchdog in him wouldn't allow Granddad's name to appear on a book cover without verifying every single fact.

He'd also hoped Sandi could steer him in the right direction to learn something of his granddad's early years in Canyon Springs. Until now, he'd never given more than a fleeting thought to how little he knew of his grandfather's past.

Macy glanced at him uneasily, Jake's indecision clearly getting on her nerves. "Is there something I can help you with?"

Or in other words, you know I can't do a thing for you so you may as well be on your way.

He'd be better off coming back later. She'd be a distraction, on top of the fact that it was unlikely he'd make much progress if he tried to poke around without Sandi's assistance. Besides, Macy might hang over his shoulder trying to see what he was doing and he wanted her to know as little about his personal life in Canyon Springs as possible. They were strangers now and he intended to keep it that way.

Then again...

"As a matter of fact, Macy—"

Chapter Five

❧

"—You can tell me why, out of all of the towns competing for your blog's attention, you chose Canyon Springs."

Macy fiddled with the photo in her fingers, then glanced up at a frowning Jake, who'd moved over to the table, and was now toying with something in his pocket.

Despite his features having matured in the years since their relationship, he looked boyishly appealing with his hair mussed from the wind. It was obvious, too, he'd cranked up his previous interest in physical fitness to an even higher level. The northland must suit him, affording opportunities for activity that went beyond a workout at the gym. His attire today reflected that outdoorsman image, with well-worn jeans, a collared shirt layered under a crewneck sweater and hiking boots. He smelled especially good when he'd walked through the door, too, mountain-fresh air clinging to him.

"I read through the applications, then separated out the ones that caught my eye." The reasons behind a decision often varied. Sometimes it was as simple as that she was tiring of travel and wanted someplace closer to St. Louis. Or maybe an application mentioned an aspect of a town she'd always wanted to know more about. Sometimes, too, a destination in critical need of spotlighting tugged at her heart.

And she always prayed.

"I narrow the field to a few," she continued. "Then I close my eyes and draw a winner."

"That sounds real scientific."

"Matters of the heart aren't necessarily scientific." His gaze held steady on hers and she wished she hadn't phrased it that way. Falling for Jake years ago hadn't had a thing to do with science, except maybe chemistry. She quickly glanced down at the photographs before her. "I have the freedom to pick and choose as I please—and as God leads."

But how much longer would she be able to do that? The more her primary sponsor became involved, the more restricted her choices might become. And if they went forward with the TV show idea, wouldn't a television network have a major say in it, too?

"So what led you to Canyon Springs specifically? What narrowed the field to include us in the eenie-meenie stage?" Resting his hands lightly on the back of a chair, he seemed determined to show her they could converse without conflict.

She motioned to her surroundings at large. "I

didn't know Arizona was anything more than sand, sun and saguaros. Pine trees? Significant snowfall? Homeowners who see little need to install air conditioning? I figured many of my readers might not know about that either. Your city council and chamber of commerce wrote a compelling proposal."

From the tiny crease still evident between his brows, Jake didn't look satisfied with her explanation. Did he think she'd tracked him down and deliberately come here to upset his world?

"So, Jake." She selected another photograph and studied the 1950s cars parked on Main Street before meeting his gaze once again. "What brought *you* to Canyon Springs? I don't remember you ever mentioning connections here."

"I guess we had more important things to be talking about."

Or doing. Like kissing. Her cheeks warmed at the memory.

His grip tightened on the back of the chair, and she got the impression he was evaluating the rest of his response. "My grandparents lived here. They were getting up in years and needed a family member close by so they could remain independent."

That seemed a CliffsNotes version of what would have been a major change in direction. Jake had never been one to make spontaneous decisions. He thought things through from all angles, weighed pros and cons, projected consequences into the future, then acted in accordance—a process that had once upon a time left her out in the cold.

"So you have roots here. That explains a lot."

"About what?"

"About why you're protective of the community." *So paranoid.* "Do your grandparents still live here?"

Another hesitation. "Grandma does. Granddad passed away last year."

"I'm sorry to hear that. Do you intend to remain here? I mean after…" When she'd first met him, he'd been a rising star with a big Phoenix legal firm, taking a temporary leave of absence to pursue an advanced degree in dispute resolution from the University of Missouri. It had been intended to bolster his professional standing as well as to lay a strong foundation for his dreamed-of future in public service. But her question hadn't come out as intended, almost insinuating that he was impatiently biding his time in a tiny town until his surviving relative departed this world and he could get on with his life.

"Canyon Springs is my home now."

He sounded sure of himself, certain of where he belonged. She envied him that. "It's quite a contrast to Phoenix," she said. "Remote. Limited opportunities."

He shrugged. "There are opportunities enough. To everything a season. It's a lifestyle I find more than agreeable."

His unmistakable glowing health testified to that,

as did the comfortable-in-his-skin confidence he'd acquired, making him more appealing than ever.

To other women, of course. Not to her.

"Where else can you go for a jog on crisp winter morning," he continued, "drive a couple of hours south to enjoy lunch on a friend's sunny patio, then come home and go cross-country skiing under a full moon that evening?"

Outdoor winter sports had never been a pursuit of hers, but it did sound fun, something she'd always wanted to explore. "It's that sort of contrast that helped me narrow the field in choosing to visit Canyon Springs. Do you camp? Fish? Horseback ride? I think those were enticements your town's application highlighted."

Jake laughed and the sound made her heart smile. "Yes, yes and yes, although I don't have a horse of my own. I borrow one or rent one. There's a local facility that stables them, and also has summer and autumn hayrides and sleighing in the winter."

His eyes brightened at the memory. Had he shared such a wintry outing with the woman she'd met at church yesterday—Paris? Her inner eye flashed unbidden to a cold, starry night. The scent of pine. The squeak of a leather harness and the jingle of bells. The brush of sleigh runners skimming through the frosty landscape as knees snuggled together under a wool Navajo blanket, the couple huddled close for warmth....

She turned back to the photographs, shaking off

the too-vivid image. She'd been enjoying the conversation with Jake entirely too much, so the reminder of Paris in the picture hadn't come a moment too soon. He'd always been easy to talk to. Interesting to listen to. That hadn't changed, and it irked her. But maybe his presence was merely evoking recollections of her carefree college days, not nostalgia for Jake himself.

He moved again to the wall of framed news articles, stopping to study the one about scholarship donors.

"Canyon Springs has its share of interesting characters, doesn't it?" He again turned toward her, his smile amiable, as if he had all the time in the world to hang out. Was he sticking around and turning on the charm to make her uncomfortable?

She looked pointedly around the museum premises, devoid of late afternoon visitors. "It would be nice to meet a few of those interesting types."

"You don't find me an interesting character?" His smile quirked and her heartbeat accelerated. *Go away, Jake.*

"I'm questioning the wisdom of arriving in Canyon Springs in April. From what everyone tells me, it's the summer months when the town hums."

"I'm surprised you don't have more control over your travel plans, your destinations." His words held a note of skepticism.

She carefully placed a fragile-looking photo on one of the piles. "It wasn't entirely my own decision. I'd intended April as a month off, with plans to fill in the blog from the archives. But my sister Nicole, who is my agent and publicist, didn't think it was a good idea. Nor did my primary sponsor."

"And you have to do whatever your sister and this sponsor want you to do?"

He'd hit a sore spot, but she managed to keep a sharp response in check. She'd hated giving up her anticipated time off. She hadn't been home for more than occasional long weekends since last summer. As much as she enjoyed the travel and her work, she had her limits.

"We discussed it and decided to keep April in my travel schedule."

"I'm more of a homebody." Jake moved to the door and grasped the knob. "Your lifestyle isn't one I'd thrive on, but I'm glad you've found something that makes you happy, Macy."

He sounded sincere, his kindhearted tone reminding her of days gone by. It was with a curious heaviness of heart that she watched him lift his hand in farewell and leave. She shook off the unwelcome feeling. Of course she'd found something that made her happy, so why should it matter whether or not it made Jake happy, too?

At nine o'clock Wednesday morning, Jake closed Macy's blog post window, pushed away from the laptop on his office desk and reached for his cell phone. He hated to bother his grandma while she was in Phoenix, but none of his research had enlightened him on his grandfather's years prior to coming to Canyon Springs.

Grandma would know the answers.

"Miss me, Jake?" He could hear the laughter in his grandmother's voice as it carried over the background ruckus of his two nieces and nephew, ages five, seven and ten. Must be a release day at their school.

"Am I interrupting anything?"

"No, Cameron's giving his sisters a hard time. Let me refill my coffee cup and step outside where it's quieter. I'll leave the door open a crack so I can still keep tabs on them."

A minute or two later he heard the door off the family room slide open and envisioned his sister and brother-in-law's ranch-style place. Typical of Sonoran desert homes, it was pale terra cotta stucco landscaped with a few orange trees and prickly pear cactus. Pale pink rhododendrons and fuchsia bougainvillea would be in bloom. It was quite a contrast to the higher elevation a few hours north, where he'd retreated after the debacle with Macy. But even in the midst of a bone-chilling snowstorm, he could honestly say he wouldn't trade what he had now for the traffic, smog and summertime heat of the Valley of the Sun.

If he eventually returned to Phoenix for professional reasons, he'd still keep his Canyon Springs home. He hadn't exaggerated when he'd told Macy the lifestyle here suited him. Grounded him. How could she tolerate that gypsylike existence?

"Ah, that's better," Grandma said. He could envision her settling in at the glass-topped table next to the pool. It would still be cool this time of day. Maybe sixty-five or so.

Seven years Granddad's junior, she'd recently celebrated her eighty-third birthday, but family members teased that she didn't look a day over seventy-five. A lively, vigorous sort who still faithfully visited the hairdresser to cloak telltale gray, she'd been active in the community until this first winter without her husband when she'd temporarily departed for the Valley.

"I'm guessing you want to talk about your grandfather's book. Am I right?"

He reached for his own mug and took a satisfied sip. Phyllis Diane made a mean cup of coffee. "As a matter of fact, I do, but not concerning the folks he documented. Did you know he didn't include anything about himself in the Canyon Springs history?"

"That's not surprising."

"Probably not. But I want to include a chapter on him—and you, of course. As a team, the two of you were instrumental in growing and developing Canyon Springs. It's easy to see what you accomplished. It's the background that's more of a blank. It was only when I sat down to put something on paper that I realized I don't know a whole lot about my own grandfather."

"What do you want to know?"

"He was born in Illinois, but do we know anything about his family besides that he was an orphan? Did he go to college or receive any professional training? Having to ask about that kind of stuff makes me feel like a self-centered jerk." He took a ragged breath. "I loved that guy and I miss him every single day. Why didn't I ask him these questions when he was alive?"

"Don't get down on yourself. Your granddad was a talker but not much about himself. I'll try to answer your questions, but I'm not sure if what I know will satisfy. He was a private man, a lot like you in that respect."

Jake pushed back in his chair. "How'd he lose his parents?"

"They died of influenza when he was two years old."

"He grew up in an orphanage, right? You'd think the sole heir of well-to-do parents would have been snatched up by a self-serving somebody before his folks were cold in the grave." The inheritance must have been a comfortable one, as when Granddad came to Canyon Springs in his early twenties, he started up a construction supply business almost immediately.

"Unfortunately, no one took him in. He never spoke of extended family."

"That's rough." Jake glanced at his grandparents' photo sitting on his desk and a heaviness settled in his chest. Both were smiling, with no evidence that Granddad had a less than advantageous start in the world. If only he himself could be half the man his grandfather had been, taking in stride whatever life handed him without whining. A man of integrity, filled with faith. "I wonder if he remembered them."

"He treasured a photograph, one of the few personal things left to him. But no, he didn't remember them."

Jake rose abruptly and moved to lean a shoulder against the wooden window frame, then took another sip of coffee as he gazed down on Main Street. "No wonder Granddad didn't care to talk about his past."

"There wasn't much to talk about. I recently found the photo in a cedar box where he kept a few personal items. His parents look extremely young. So sad."

"It is." Deep in thought, Jake studied the street below. "What about after his childhood, but before he came out West? He'd have been old enough to serve in World War II, wouldn't he?"

"You know he was severely injured when he was younger."

Jake nodded, recalling his grandfather's left eye, scarred and permanently sealed closed. Long sleeves usually concealed healed-over burns on his arms, but the severe limp remained a constant reminder.

"As I recall," she continued, "it was the result of an explosion or something of that nature when he was in his late teens and working around heavy equipment. He never mentioned military duty and I've never seen paperwork to that effect, so I assume those injuries kept him out of the service."

"Not an easy thing to swallow, I'm sure, by a man who loved his country as he did."

Glimpsing a sun-dappled sheen of long blond hair, Jake suddenly straightened at the window as a trim, energetic figure crossed the street below. Macy, in jeans and a light jacket, waved at someone just out of sight. Who?

He cringed as the volume of childish voices at his sister's house escalated in the background. He might need to rethink that invitation to have the kids come up for a couple of long weekends this summer as they'd done in the past.

"Sounds as if I'd better go break that up, Jake. Your sister is grocery shopping, so I'm in charge this morning. I don't want this ruckus to become a 911 episode. If you think of other questions, call back later."

"You don't mind? I know you miss Granddad even more than I do." He shifted at the window to see where Macy was heading. "I don't want to make it more painful by making you talk about him."

"Nothing can make it more painful." Her words came wistfully. "I think about him constantly, and talking about him is a joy. Too often people try to divert me from speaking of him, insisting I shouldn't, as they say, 'dwell on my loss.'"

"You can talk about him to me anytime you want, Gran. I only wish I hadn't been focused on myself all those years. Then maybe I'd have more answers to my questions."

"I think your grandfather told us everything he wanted us to know about him, Jake. At times I sensed there was an underlying sadness about him. Something from before I knew him. The loss of his parents, certainly. But maybe regret, too. When I'd question him, he'd merely smile that smile of his and assure me all was right in his world. How could it be anything less, he'd insist, with God giving him such a beautiful wife to put up with him?"

"He really loved you."

"I know he did. And he loved you, too. Was proud of you." She paused as though considering her next words. "I pray someday you'll find the kind of love that the two of us shared, Jake."

"Me, too." But he wasn't holding his breath. He'd once been sure he'd found his Mrs. Right, but somehow he'd misread God's intentions. How did a guy know for certain he was hearing from heaven and not solely following his own desires?

When he'd shut off the phone, he craned his neck to see who Macy was speaking with outside the local bakery.

His fingers tightened around the coffee mug as recognition dawned.

Cate Landreth. Town gossip extraordinaire. What Cate didn't know about the residents of this town could fit on the head of a pin. He'd heard it said, too, that she made up what she didn't know to be a fact. She'd be a fount of insider information on the locals and not a bit shy about sharing it.

He shifted for a better angle to observe them. But when the two chatting females turned to enter the bakery together, he set his mug on the wooden windowsill with a thump.

Then he shot out the door past a startled Phyllis Diane and headed to the stairs.

Chapter Six

"No, I hadn't heard that about them, Cate." Macy breathed in the tantalizing scent of fresh-baked muffins, doughnuts and sweet breads as she answered the woman standing beside her. She'd met Bill Diaz, owner of the Lazy D Campground and RV Park, but didn't know he had a romance going with Sharon Dixon, the Dix's Woodland Warehouse proprietor with whom she'd soon be working. If there was any truth to Cate's gossip, and depending on the stage of their relationship, maybe Sharon and Bill would let her feature them on the blog, another romantic story to entice her readers.

"Everybody in town wants Sharon to find some happiness." The auburn-haired Cate nodded knowingly as she pointed out a chocolate-drenched éclair to the white-clad clerk, her red-lacquered nails glinting in the light. From behind the display the young woman secured the pastry with tongs and placed it on a decorative paper plate. "She's had a rough life.

Husband ran off. Had to raise her daughter by herself. Then she's had health problems on top of it all. But things are looking up for her now. You know, heating up in the romance department."

Cate exchanged a few dollars for the decadent breakfast delight, then winked at the clerk. "Isn't that right, Denise?"

The young woman smiled uncertainly, as if unsure of the facts—or maybe questioning the wisdom in agreeing to them. From the moment she'd met Cate at Kit's yesterday, Macy suspected her to be a gossipmonger. She seemed too eager to share the private concerns of her neighbors and exhibited more interest in Macy's personal life than Macy was comfortable sharing with a stranger. Cate had peppered her with prying questions, starting with a blatant "why aren't you married?" It made Macy uncomfortable... and uncertain about listening to all the stories the woman had to share.

But try as she might, Macy didn't know how to wiggle out of a bakery visit this morning without appearing rude.

She acquired her own doughnut, and they'd seated themselves at a bistro table in the back when the bells above the entrance jingled. She placed her doughnut and coffee on the table across from Cate, then glanced toward the front of the shop.

Just the sight of Jake, looking amazingly attractive this morning in black trousers and a gray polo shirt, sent her heart racing. Residual crush, that's all it was, right? An echo from the past. Nothing more.

As he waited to be served at the counter, Cate gave her a pointed look and nodded discreetly toward the new arrival.

"Bachelor," Cate whispered under her breath, then bit into her éclair.

Macy didn't respond, but it was evident from the lingering looks in his direction that the other woman approved of the view. Macy kept her face turned away from him, concentrating on unfolding her napkin and arranging the items in front of her. When he finally noticed her sitting with what she suspected was a town gossip, she had no doubt that he'd come charging over to read her the riot act. Maybe if she didn't draw his attention, she could postpone that moment a little longer.

Cate slowly licked her lips, then took a sip of coffee, her gaze never leaving Jake as he placed an order. "He's a real catch. Attorney. Never married, although I know more than a few who are doing their best to land him."

Paris Perslow? It was tempting to ask, but she wasn't sure she wanted to know the answer. If anyone in town was suited to Jake, it would be the exquisite Paris.

"You should throw your hat in the ring." Cate momentarily drew her attention from Jake to give Macy a sly smile. "Have you met?"

Macy's face warmed under Cate's scrutiny. "Yes, we've met, but I don't think—"

"Good morning, Jake," Cate called out. "So what do you think of our pretty *Hometowns With Heart* visitor?"

Macy cringed as Jake's head jerked in their direction, but she managed a wan smile as their gazes met. The clerk handed him his change and he reached for a white, cellophane-windowed box, then headed to their table.

"Good morning, Cate. Macy." He looked down at the pair, his smile friendly, with no evidence he suspected Macy of colluding with a rumormonger. But she knew better. He jiggled the box in his hand and she glimpsed a variety of sugary temptations. "It looks as if you ladies have the same craving I do for a tasty morning treat."

Macy stared at him. Jake craving sweets? A rare bagel with fat-free cream cheese, maybe. But never pastries.

"Since when—" His eyes met hers with unexpected directness and she cut herself off. They'd agreed not to let it be known they shared a past and she'd almost blown it in front of an eagle-eyed Cate. "I mean, you don't look like someone who's into indulging."

Had he seen her coming here with Cate and concocted this uncharacteristic yen for sweets in order to spy on her?

Jake proudly slapped his flat midsection, accepting her comment as a compliment. "No, I don't often give in, but it's not easy to resist when picking up something to share at the office."

"I was telling Macy—" Cate's eyes darted from Jake to her and back again with a speculative gleam "—that this same spot has been a bakery for fifty years."

"It has indeed." He nodded in Macy's direction. "Interviewing the newest owners, a third generation of bakers, might make for a nice touch on your blog. They have great recipes, too, if you can get them to turn loose of a few."

"Wonderful idea. Thanks," she said as she toyed with her untouched cup. Was he going to stand there all morning to make sure she didn't—how was it he put it?—lead someone down a breadcrumb-strewn path to disclosing the secret lives, loves and vices of Canyon Springs residents? She had a feeling it wouldn't take much to pry that kind of information out of her new acquaintance, who seemed to enjoy randomly scattering juicy tidbits in hopes Macy would ask to sample more.

Already this morning, in the ten or so minutes before they'd come inside the bakery, she'd heard of the former spouses of both Bill and Sharon taking off for new adventures and tales of Rob McGuire's and Bryce Harding's questionable pasts.

Jake cleared his throat. "Well, I guess I'd better be on my way."

"I'm sure your coworkers eagerly await your delivery." She'd give anything to see the reaction of his office mates when he toted in the bakery goods. She guessed he would be met with unconcealed surprise.

He glanced up at the wall clock, then down at her. "Aren't you starting at Dix's today?"

So he *had* been looking at her schedule and knew of her rapidly approaching start time. "I am. But I still have a few minutes left to finish here."

"I'd be happy to walk you over and introduce you to the owner."

Dix's was only a few doors down, wasn't it? "Thanks, but I met Sharon at church. I imagine we'll remember each other."

A crease between Jake's brows deepened, and she couldn't help but smile inwardly. As she'd suspected, he'd come in the shop solely to ensure she didn't talk too long with Cate. Did he have any idea how transparent he was?

"Let the girl eat in peace, Jake." Cate had finished her pastry and carefully wiped her fingertips on a napkin, amusement lighting her eyes. "If you want to spend more time with her, be a man and spit out an invitation to dinner."

His brows shot up.

"Oh, I don't think—" Macy shook her head in apology for Cate's audacity.

"I'm sure she's up to her neck in dinner invitations," Jake mumbled. "I wouldn't want to—"

"No, no, of course not." Macy again fiddled with her cup.

Jake nodded in obvious relief, then stepped away from the table, the pastry box gripped tightly enough to sustain a permanent dent. "I'll see you ladies later."

Macy watched him out the door, then turned to an openly grinning Cate. "What?"

The older woman settled back in her chair, studying Macy with an assessing gleam in her eyes. "This is going to be one mighty interesting month."

"What do you mean?"

"Didn't you see that? The tips of Jake's ears turning pink?" Cate let out a cackling laugh, then leaned forward conspiratorially. "That man might have high-tailed it out of here at record speed when I put him on the spot, but don't fool yourself. You've shaken him up but good, Miss Macy Colston. Take advantage of it and you might finally get your hands on a husband."

A husband? She wasn't looking for a husband. And she'd certainly learned the hard way not to look in Jake's direction for one.

He should have known it would only be a matter of time before Cate Landreth positioned herself to be a resource for Macy, probably hoping to be featured in one of the daily blog posts. But what was it with Cate zeroing in on *him* yesterday morning, trying to set him up with Macy?

Disgruntled, Jake wandered into the kitchen to rummage for something to call supper. Abe, toenails clicking on the tiled floor, followed at his heels. The beagle never received scraps at dinnertime, not even as a pup, but he never lost hope.

Maybe that was a spiritual insight people needed to learn from their dogs?

With Abe flopped at his feet, Jake ate his warmed-up hamburger and paged through a photocopy of Granddad's book. He couldn't bring himself to mark up the original version painstakingly typed on an ancient manual Remington. He had Phyllis Diane converting the original manuscript into an electronic document so the editing process could start in earnest.

There was still so much he didn't know about Granddad's pre-Canyon Springs days. Nevertheless, he and Grandma made a significant contribution to the town, every bit as much as the Falkners, Perslows and Odels, who'd put down roots before the arrival of Jake's own family. That's what an additional chapter in the history book could focus on. In their sixty-five years of marriage, they'd helped make the town what it was today.

Wow. Sixty-five years. That boggled his mind.

I pray someday you'll find the kind of love that the two of us shared, Jake.

Grandma's words echoed through his mind and he shifted his feet restlessly, accidentally kicking Abe. "Sorry, bud."

The pup wagged his tail, a wet nose sniffing expectantly as if a long-awaited treat might be bestowed as recompense.

Jake crunched a single too-salty chip. If he'd spoken up years ago, gotten his feelings in the open, could he have circumvented the chain of events leading to his and Macy's breakup?

No, that was wishful thinking. His caution had proven to be well-placed. Most of that spring of her senior year she'd been working behind the scenes—behind *his* back—taking what he'd shared with her about his accountant friend's dilemma and turning it into a news story to launch her career. If he'd been more open with his feelings, her betrayal would only have hurt more.

His cell phone vibrated and he reached for it, glancing at the caller ID. Larry James, fellow councilman.

"Hey, Lar, what's up?" Larry was Don's younger brother by five years, a mustached version of his curly-haired sibling.

"I got a call this afternoon from Merle Perslow inquiring about the availability of that piece of property your granddad gave the city."

"He's interested in buying it?" Merle was Paris's father, a successful regional real estate agent. If it came to the town selling off the place, it would be far better for a local to acquire it rather than an outsider.

"Naw. Some California-based chain—a yogurt place or something—is interested in the land, not the house."

"A chain, huh?" And they weren't interested in the house, only the property it sat on. Which meant they'd raze Grandma and Granddad's first home in Canyon Springs. The old stone bungalow, nestled on a few wooded acres not far from the historical museum, would be replaced with a parking lot and cookie-cutter construction.

A muscle in Jake's neck tightened. Why had Granddad not left the property to his wife, daughter or grandkids? He'd considered contesting the will, but Grandma had talked him out of it, saying she respected her life partner's wishes even after he was gone.

"I know what you're thinking, Jake," Larry continued, "but not many locals have the kind of money the town needs to ask for the place. Once the council makes the final decision to sell, we may have to look beyond the city limits for a buyer. We can't let it go for a song."

"You know I'm trying to come up with the money."

If only he hadn't turned down Granddad's offer to cut him a deal on it when he'd first moved here. But leery of the major remodel required, he'd instead bought a newly constructed home. Who would have thought Granddad would divest himself of the property altogether? Jake cringed at the possibility his indifference to it might have saddened his grandfather.

"I'm not going to get too shaken up just yet." Jake looped his arm over the back of the kitchen chair, his casual words belying the concern that gnawed in his belly. "If Merle's honest with that California company, they'll learn real quick that Canyon Springs only booms three to four months out of the year. A lot of locals close up shop entirely during the off-season, but they're not trying to earn a return for investors."

"Maybe." Larry didn't sound convinced. "Anyway, I'll be informing the council at next week's meeting that there's been a promising inquiry about your grandpa's place."

"I appreciate your letting me know. See you next week."

"Oh, um, Jake?" He could picture Larry brushing down the corner of his mustache with his fingertip.

"Yeah?"

"If you want to borrow a mountain bike—" Larry cleared his throat "—just holler. Won't cost you a dime. On the house."

Larry owned a sports rental shop. Bikes, cross-country skis, snowboards and sleds. All sorts of outdoor gear. But why did he think Jake would want to borrow a mountain bike? "Thanks, but I already have one."

"I know, but if you'd need, you know, two…"

"Don't need two, Larry." Was he missing something here?

"No, I guess not. I thought…no, never mind."

When they finished, Jake set aside his phone and glanced down at Abe. "If it's not one thing, it's another, isn't it?"

He had pressing client matters to attend to, book research and revisions to complete, and now he had to concern himself with some California chain pushing to get their hands on Granddad's old place.

Oh, and then there was Macy. Always Macy.

If only his friend Patrick hadn't delayed coming forth as a whistleblower. New to the job, he'd gotten sucked into doing things he felt he shouldn't. Jake had advised him to retain legal counsel in his own state and then go forward to the authorities, but his suggestion had gone unheeded.

That, however, didn't justify Macy's betrayal of a confidence. Would he ever forget Patrick's call? The accusing tone that sent him dashing to a quick-stop shop for a copy of the *St. Louis Post-Dispatch?* His friend insisted he'd spoken to no one but him and the byline of the scathing article was the name of the woman he knew Jake was dating.

Abe pressed his nose against his master's leg and Jake leaned down to rub the furry head, the long velvety ears brushing his fingers. "Yes, I forgave Macy a long time ago, so don't go thinking I'm still holding it against her."

She'd not only been young, but young in the faith. Unfortunately, her arrival in Canyon Springs stirred up uncomfortable memories. Too-pleasant ones, as well.

"I'm sunk, Abe. I thought I was over her, but…" He shook his head. The sound of her voice still melted his heart. Her laughter held him captive. The generous smile reminded him of how she'd enthusiastically stop to chat with strangers during Sunday afternoon excursions. Always curious. Always questioning. A city girl through and through, she'd nevertheless been drawn to rural towns. People responded warmly to her interest, which, of course, made her and the blog an ideal fit.

Odd, though, that she hadn't pursued the investigative journalism avenue after such an auspicious start. Knowing the depth of her ambition—and that of her overbearing mother—there had to be a story behind the abrupt change in direction.

Jake stood and gave himself a mental shake. He had to stop dwelling on the what-ifs of the past. God shut the door firmly years ago, so who was he to contemplate prying it open again? Monday afternoon he'd had Phyllis Diane pick up Macy's schedule from the chamber office, thinking by consulting it he could ensure there would be no future accidental run-ins that would make them both uncomfortable.

But yesterday morning's episode at the bakery proved that avoiding her would mean more opportunities for her to have encounters such as he'd caught her in with Cate. Although he disliked the thought of it, maybe he should put the information about her schedule to a more strategic use—like keeping tabs on her as she'd already accused him of doing. How else could he make certain she wasn't up to something he and his town might come to regret?

Chapter Seven

Thank goodness Jake had kept himself scarce the past few days. Or at least if he *was* spying on her, he was doing it from afar. So why did her spirits sink each time the bell above the door at Dix's Woodland Warehouse jingled and a stranger walked in? Or steps sounded on the porch at the historical museum, but it wasn't Jake?

She wasn't disappointed not to see him—that would be crazy. She'd asked him to keep his distance and he was honoring that. Cate's talk that she'd "shaken him up but good" might be true, but not romantically as Cate had interpreted.

Just as she'd opened a box of sweatshirts—one of her volunteer assignments was stocking shelves at the store—Macy's cell phone played its distinctive tune. She snatched it from her blazer pocket. "Hey, Ava. What's up?"

"You love giving me challenges, don't you?"

With a laugh, Macy looked around the empty

store. Would this place soon be buzzing as promised? "What now?"

"That Dexter Smith you gave me? Bad enough he's
a Smith, but I looked him up and he's dead."

She snorted, loving Ava's sense of humor. "Don't
tell me you're surprised. From the age he looked to
be in the 1960s photo, he'd be—what? Late eighties?
Early nineties?"

"It's not a surprise he's no longer living," Ava said,
her tone dry. "I mean he's dead *twice*. He passed on
last year *and* in 1941. December 7, 1941, to be exact."

"Pearl Harbor?"

"That's my guess."

Macy shrugged. "There's probably been a billion
men in the world named Dexter Smith."

"Plenty. But not many Dexter *Canton* Smiths. You
can see, can't you, what I'm up against with him?
Now this other gal is a different story." Ava's voice
rang with satisfaction. "I should have something on
her for you soon."

Macy pulled a forest green "Canyon Springs"
sweatshirt from the box and placed it on a small
oak table, her fingers lingering on the soft, cottony
fabric. "Thanks, my friend. God sure knew what He
was doing when we met on that elevator."

"Yes, ma'am. He did."

They closed the call with plans to touch base in a
day or two. Macy had finished unboxing the sweatshirts when the familiar tinkle of bells announced
a customer. She tamped down the silly fluttering

hope that it might be Jake, then turned to welcome the newcomer.

Her breath caught.

"Good morning, Macy." Jake glanced around as he strolled toward her. "Is Sharon here?"

"She's in the office. Would you like me to get her?"

"I can find my way back there, thanks."

But he didn't make a move in that direction. Was he here to check up on her? She tried to read his expression as he studied the interior of the general store, taking in the raftered ceiling, wide-planked floor and cozy iron woodstove. Neatly stocked shelves of grocery and household items shared space with outdoor gear.

He eyed the stack of sweatshirts and the empty box on the floor. "How do you like working here? I got a kick out of it a couple of summers when I was a teenager."

"You worked here as a kid? I thought you didn't move to town until after you got your degree in dispute resolution from MU."

"I moved here permanently at that time. But I lived here in second grade with my mom and sister after my folks divorced. Mom relocated us to the Valley again after that, but I came back most summers through high school."

"I had no idea." She'd known his parents divorced when he'd been young, but he'd never talked about his growing-up years. No wonder he was attached to Canyon Springs. She should have wondered how a city boy could fit so comfortably into those Sunday afternoon jaunts they'd taken through the tiny burgs of mid-Missouri. He had some small-town boy rooted deep inside him.

He was the one who'd launched her fascination for those hometowns with heart the autumn they'd met. He'd stroll along at her side, uncomplaining when she'd pull out her camera for a shot of a quaint shop window or garden gate. He'd shake his head in amused tolerance when she'd quiz a local woman on the details of her candle-making business or ask for a recipe at an out-of-the-way restaurant. He'd chime in on occasion with a few insightful questions of his own, then offer her a discreet wink. If he had a problem with her blog now, he had only himself to thank for lighting that spark in her in the first place.

Get your head out of the past, girl. But it wasn't easy with Jake standing in front of her, forcing to the surface details of their relationship she thought she'd long forgotten. "To answer your question, yes, I'm enjoying working here even though the promised summer tourist traffic is a ways off."

He cocked a brow in mock disapproval. "Seasonal guests are what the more politically correct prefer to call them."

"My faux pas." She couldn't help but smile. "But tourists or not, it does sound as if summer in Canyon Springs is the place to be if you're looking for a slower pace."

Jake laughed. "For visitors maybe. But for townspeople, summertime is when things start humming. The whole economy depends on money flowing in from Memorial Day through Labor Day, so we hustle to keep everyone happy."

"Well, look who's here early on a Friday morning." With the husky tone of a former smoker, Sharon Dixon's cheerful greeting carried to the front of the store as she made her way up an aisle. The auburn-haired woman in her mid-fifties gave Jake a teasing smile. "My pretty new assistant has proven to be a drawing card."

"He's here to see *you*, Sharon." Macy placed a sweatshirt on a nearby shelf.

"That's what all these young men say when I catch them stopping by. But don't think I haven't noticed the increase in foot traffic since you started. You're good for business, doll." Eyes twinkling, she turned to Jake. "So what's on your mind? You're not here to tell me the city's increasing property taxes again, are you?"

"No, ma'am. I wouldn't dare. You'd throw me out on the street before I could get the words out of my mouth."

Sharon gave a brisk nod. "You're right about that."

"Actually, I'm doing a poll of business owners."

"And it requires a personal visit? Email or a phone call wouldn't do?" She winked at Macy, not realizing his presence was unrelated to any attraction to her. "Gotta hand it to this gentleman, Macy, he always goes that extra mile."

"I'm sure he does."

Jake's brow creased, no doubt remembering how she'd scolded him for being too diligent in his studies. The small-town outings they'd taken on the weekends had been his proof that he could loosen up. As with everything else he did, he'd thrown his heart into making his point, going as far as adopting a puppy, with her encouragement. Did he still have Abe? Did he allow himself to have any fun at all?

"As you're more than aware, Sharon," Jake said with a sympathetic look, "the downturn in the economy has left Canyon Springs struggling."

"Which is why we brought in Macy here. To give us a boost." She nodded approvingly in Macy's direction.

See, Jake? Not everyone thinks I'm a bad guy.

"That's one step taken. Publicity never hurts. But while it gives a temporary boost to a city's bottom line, it almost never provides a long-term solution."

He gave Macy a pointed look almost as if to remind her she'd be here today and gone tomorrow. Three weeks from now Canyon Springs—and Jake—would go on without her.

Which is exactly what she wanted, too, wasn't it?

"So what's the long-term solution, doll?" Concern lit Sharon's eyes as she looked to Jake. "I hear the council may sell property the city was bequeathed. Of course, you know all about that."

He did. But he didn't want to talk about it in front

of Macy. She'd try to turn it into a feature story on her blog, playing up council members at odds on what to do with the property willed to the town. He himself would be right smack in the middle of the controversy, not a place he cared to be in a popular national forum. Man, it got tiring having to always take his image into consideration. He'd been doing it for so long it was second nature, but sometimes...

He kept his tone even. "That would be a stop-gap measure, too, unfortunately. No, I'm here to ask how you'd feel about strengthening your sponsorship of local kids in non sports-related activities. Art, pho-tography, writing, general physical fitness."

Sharon's mouth took a downward turn. "We cut a bunch of those programs last year, didn't we? The ones that don't draw cheering crowds."

Jake nodded. "Not by choice, and we hoped it would only be temporary. But I don't see that we can reinstate much this coming summer."

"That's a shame."

"Which is why I'm approaching local businesses about—"

"Wait!" Macy snapped her fingers, her eyes bright. "What if we do a fund-raiser while I'm here? We could hold an event and charge an admission fee."

He caught the "we," but cast an indulgent smile her way. She had no idea of the time, effort and expense something like that entailed. "That's a nice idea for on down the road. You know, when there's time to drum up support and develop a plan, but—"

"Why not now?" she challenged. "Before summer so you can keep more of your programs? You're thinking way too elaborate, Jake. Go for something simple and quick to plan. Maybe a dessert night. Bring in a high school choir, gussy up the tables, turn down the lights and voilà! You're set for an elegant evening at twenty-five dollars a head."

Sharon nodded. "That's a good idea, doll. We do similar things around the winter holidays, but warmer weather usually gives way to barbecues and picnics."

"I think it's still too chilly for outdoor events." Macy rubbed her hands up and down her arms. Her attire still appeared more geared to the lower elevations than the high country, but he noticed she'd made do with light sweaters and had found herself a pair of closed-toe shoes.

"I don't know…." He hated to be negative, but he could see this being a big flop. Like the time he and his Canyon Springs grade school buddies created a backyard game carnival. They put up a tent under Grandma's clothesline, blew up balloons and spent their allowances on candy prizes. Nobody came. "I think we'd need something more to draw a crowd than the high school choir."

Macy tossed back her hair and pointed to herself. "Me."

He stifled a grin. "You sing and dance, do you? Put on a show?"

"Go ahead, laugh, Mr. Councilman. But towns do

things like this when I visit. Surely you've read about them on my blog."

On the lookout for any signs of misbehavior on her part, he must have only skimmed over irrelevant details in her posts.

Sharon nodded again. "I remember reading about them."

He pursed his lips. "People donate twenty-five dollars a head to meet you and have a piece of pie?"

She lifted her chin. "Fifty. A hundred even. Sometimes more to sit at the head table with me."

"You're kidding."

"No, I'm not." She drew back in pretended offense. "Lending my name and presence gets people's attention. I think of it as my ministry. I know it's hard for you to grasp with my only claim to fame being a professional blogger, but people *like* to meet me."

He motioned to the door. "They can walk in here and talk to you for free anytime. Why would they want to fork over—"

"I think we should do it." Sharon spoke emphatically, her eyes resting on Macy. "I'm in favor of the dessert idea. Every woman in town and a few of the men, too, will have a family favorite they'd be willing to donate."

They were getting ahead of themselves. Not thinking this through. "Now, ladies, let's don't go—"

Sharon cut him a sharp look. "Why not? You came in here to drum up funds for kids programs, didn't you? Now here you have your answer but you're look-ing a gift horse in the mouth."

"You are, Jake," Macy chimed in, her eyes twin-kling at his discomfort with the idea.

Sharon gave a decisive nod. "Paris Perslow could throw together something like this in no time flat. Blindfolded even."

Jake held up a hand. "Now hold on, I'm not ask-ing Paris to get involved."

Sharon frowned. "Then I will, doll."

"Come on, Jake," Macy wheedled. "I'm more than willing to be a part of it, to help out in any way I can. I love giving back to the towns that welcome me with open arms."

Sharon nudged him. "You hear that? She thinks we've welcomed her with open arms. Don't go giv-ing her the impression that might not be the case."

"Smart move on the fund-raiser," Macy's mother, Trina Colston, said approvingly when they talked after dinner the following evening. "Good promo for the blog. Do you think this councilman and Paris per-son can pull it off so quickly? That's not much time."

No, it wasn't. A barefooted Macy scooted back on the lodge's bed to rest against a bank of cushiony pillows. She'd initially been about as thrilled as Jake seemed when Sharon suggested Paris be in-volved. She herself couldn't get too excited about showcasing Paris's acclaimed talents, but couldn't at the time imagine what the source of Jake's reluctance might be.

Now, however, looking across the room at a festive springtime flower arrangement that had been delivered to her room, she suspected he and Ms. Perslow had parted ways. What else could the flowers and his accompanying note mean? True, the tone of the note didn't quite sound like him…but the note identified him as the sender. It left her confused—and tingling with curiosity.

Did Jake feel the same attraction for her that she was feeling for him? No, that was ridiculous. They already knew a relationship between them could never work. They were just too different.

Now all she had to do was convey that to the butterflies in her stomach….

"It's going to be simple, Mom. High school gymnasium. Donated desserts. Maybe a school choir or orchestra."

"I wish it could be something more upscale." No doubt Mom was comparing it to last winter's affair at her country club. Ice sculptures. A harpist. Shimmering gowns and black tuxes. Macy enjoyed the evening with her parents and their friends, but could honestly say she'd be equally as comfortable eating homemade pie in a high school gym for a good cause.

"It may not be ritzy, but I assure you it will be a fun evening."

"I suppose." Macy could picture her mother thoughtfully nibbling on her lower lip. "What is your plan to meet your sponsor's request for the blog's content? I assume you're working up something beyond a rehash of that saccharine sweet trio of holiday weddings and the horses at church. Who names a horse Taco anyway?"

Not surprisingly, Mom was monitoring her every online word. A muscle in Macy's shoulder tightened. "I have several ideas."

"You've been there a week and you only have ideas?"

She again gazed at the floral arrangement across the room. She could hardly say she'd been distracted by a certain city councilman who had her reevaluating every idea she came up with. The pressure for something spectacular this month to impress the sponsor didn't help either. Topics that would have been enjoyably written now seemed dull and lifeless in the light of the expectations of those around her.

"Blogging is an art form," she assured her, her eyes lingering on the daisy-carnation-lily mix. "I don't want to crowd my muse."

She never thought she'd be a victim of writer's block, but last night she'd barely eked out this morning's post. Even worse, at the moment her mind was a total blank for tomorrow's. Jake was watching to make sure she *didn't* compromise anyone in his town and her family and sponsor were looking over her shoulder hoping she *would*. No wonder she couldn't think of anything to say!

Her mother's sigh carried over the phone. "Don't

wait too long for this so-called inspiration. As a journalist I found the best muse in the business is to sit your fanny down at the keyboard and get to work."

Macy slid off the bed and crossed the room to where the flowers rested on the desk. She closed her eyes and bent to breathe in the calming floral scent. Her mother hadn't done anything remotely journalistic in thirty-five years, but Macy had learned not to argue.

"Don't worry, Mom, it's under control."

"I certainly hope so. Everyone is counting on you."

When they'd said their goodbyes, she shut off her phone and again leaned over to inhale the sweet scent of the blossoms. Then she removed the printed card from the foliage and read it for the hundredth time.

Chapter Eight

He'd drop off the fund-raiser proposal and be on his way. He didn't need to linger, Jake reminded himself as he stood in the corridor outside Macy's room at Kit's Lodge. But she didn't answer the door. Maybe she hadn't returned from the Saturday night dinner with a Canyon Springs family he'd seen on her schedule.

She seemed plenty popular with this hometown crowd, which wasn't surprising. Although she was still the direct, determined Macy he'd known in Missouri, she seemed somehow different, too. More mellow? More at peace? Or was that *him* who'd found a deeper level of inner quiet in the half dozen years since they'd parted ways? All he knew was the briefest moment spent with her was like receiving an injection of renewed energy and anticipatory promise.

Which was crazy. God hadn't given him any green lights. Not so much as a flashing yellow.

He knocked again, with no response. Maybe he'd

leave the envelope at the front desk. But as he was about to turn away, he heard the chain lock clatter and the deadbolt turn. Then there she was, her long hair spilling over her shoulders and eyes bright with an unexpected *something* that ramped up his heart rate. Whoa. Was that a speculative gleam of interest?

"This is a surprise, Jake."

He wouldn't argue with that. She hadn't looked at him like that in a long time. Not sure what to make of it, he self-consciously held out the envelope. "This is a draft of Sharon's and Paris's ideas for the proposed fund-raiser. You can see if it's similar to what you've found to be successful elsewhere."

She opened the envelope and scanned the typed page, then smiled at him. "This is perfect. Absolutely perfect. I can't believe your friends jumped on this so quickly."

"Had to. You only have three more weeks here and the Friday prior to your last week is when the high school gym is available." He stuffed his hands in his jacket pockets. "Thanks for offering to help us out."

"I'm more than happy to."

He stood for a moment longer, taking in her India-style printed tunic and jeans, with no socks or shoes. "In spite of our weather, you're still the sandals and barefoot gal I remember."

She glanced down and laughed, then looked up at him almost shyly, a questioning look in her eyes. "I guess I am."

Not sure what to make of her behavior, he stepped

back. "I don't want to take up your time. It's getting late and I imagine you have a blog to write tonight."

"I do." She studied him uncertainly. "But do you have a minute? I have something to show you."

Curious, he followed when she motioned him into the room, then pushed the door not-quite-shut behind them. He'd seen accommodations at Kit's before, although he'd never stayed there himself. He was familiar with the mountain-themed interior, but somehow Macy managed to put her own stamp on her surroundings. She'd arranged a portable office on the small oak desk and placed a well-worn Bible on the nightstand. Beside it sat a framed motto he remembered from Macy's dorm room.

Stop Chasing Butterflies.

He tensed at the command. That said it all, epitomizing the narrow focus and single-minded determination he'd belatedly come to recognize. With effort, he drew his gaze away from the haunting words, conscious that the room even smelled like her citrusy scent, blending with a whiff of…fresh flowers? A small card poked up through the foliage of a ribboned floral arrangement sitting on the desk.

Who sent her flowers?

"I have a dilemma," she said, picking up a handful of index cards and handing them to him. "Look at these."

He flipped through the recipes and cracked a smile. "Slow-cooker roast? This is one of the few things I can cook without messing up too badly."

She moved closer and he again breathed in the enticing scent that was all Macy. "These are five recipes given to me by five different ladies hoping theirs will be featured in my food section. Each told me it was an *old* family recipe. You know, it's been around for generations, practically roasted over an open campfire in their kin's pioneering past."

"So what's the problem?" Man, did she ever smell good. "Can't you put more than one recipe in your blog? I imagine there are lots of different ways to do a roast in a slow cooker."

She took the cards from his hand, fanned them out in her own, then held them so he could see them plainly. "Look more closely, Jake. They're the *same* recipe. Identical, right down to the details."

Still conscious of her proximity, he forced himself to focus word for word on the cards, all jotted down in a variety of distinctive handwriting styles. "Well, I'll be."

"They each told me the recipe is a family secret, but because they admire *Hometowns With Heart* they're willing to share with my readers."

"Secret family recipe, huh?" He glanced at the names on the cards, then quirked a smile. "I didn't realize all these people were related. That's a small town for you."

"Very funny." She snatched the cards away. "I guess I could list everyone's name, give them all credit."

That got his attention. "Credit for the same secret family recipe? Do you want to start a war?"

She looked up at him, her brows an inverted V. "I was afraid you'd say that."

"It won't go over well, Macy, I can guarantee you that."

"So what should I do?"

She was asking him? Wanting his input? "Find another recipe. Search the web for an alternative. Use mine if you have to." Then he thought better of that idea. "Don't use my name, though, okay?"

"Oh, I don't know…" Again he got the sense that there was a question on the tip of her tongue, but she held it back and gave him a teasing smile. "It might add a new dimension to your image. You know, similar to candidates who claim the best barbecue sauce in the state or award-winning brownies. A nice down-home touch, don't you think? Or is a future in state politics no longer on your agenda?"

"It's still on the agenda, but I'll pass on the image enhancement, thanks." He took the index cards from her once again and riffled through them. "How'd they end up with the same secret family recipe? Even Paris."

"I'm guessing it appeared in a popular women's magazine fifty years or so ago and was then transcribed by their mothers or grandmothers and dropped into the recipe file. Instant family tradition."

He frowned. "Maybe I should ask Paris."

"Absolutely not." Her soft, manicured hands pried the cards from his, then placed them on the desk—next to the flowers. "We don't want to ruin family folklore. Give me your recipe. Hopefully it's not another twin to these."

"It's not." He plunged his hands into his pockets to keep from reaching out to touch the silken strands of her hair. "I made it up a few years ago with what I found in the pantry. None of these call for a couple of cans of tomato soup poured over the roast. But you won't use my name or photo, right?"

She nodded with mock solemnity. "I promise."

"Thanks." He stared down at her a too-long moment, then abruptly turned to the door. He needed a drink of cold mountain air to clear his head of the effect she had on him. Nevertheless, he paused as curiosity got the best of him. "Nice flowers."

"More than nice." Was she blushing? Who sent her those posies? "I have to admit, Jake, considering the history between us, these took me by surprise. You never sent me flowers before. Thank you."

Her luminous green eyes tentatively searched his. What was she talking about? He hadn't sent her any flowers now either.

She stepped to the arrangement and pulled the small card from the greenery, silently reading the words. Then she looked to him again. "I take it I misunderstood your relationship with Paris Perslow?"

He swallowed, still confused. "Paris?"

She nodded. "I was under the impression when you introduced us at the church last weekend that you were seeing each other."

Where'd she get that idea? Her newfound friend,

Cate? But it didn't matter at the moment. Right now he only cared why Macy thought he'd sent her flowers. She raised her brows in expectation of his response as he debated whether or not to tell her they weren't from him.

"No, we're not seeing each other." He sidled closer to Macy, hoping to catch a glimpse of the card's message.

Her eyes brightened as she leaned over to inhale the scent of the colorful blossoms. "I feel better about these then. And about the note. The sentiment was, to say the least, unexpected."

What did the note say? Give me a hint, Macy. "That's me. Mr. Spontaneity."

Eyes sparkling, she laughed as she shook the card in his face. "You don't have a spontaneous bone in your body and you know it."

"I don't know about that. Let's take a look at this." Helpless but to return her smile, he slipped the card from her fingers and held it out for inspection. The words on the imprinted cardstock were computer-generated. No handwritten signature. But the message was loud and clear, "Lovely Lady—Where Have You Been All My Life? Jake."

Warmth rushed up his neck. Good grief.

The local florist was none other than city council member Bernice Cruz. Why did Bernie permit someone to send Macy flowers and a cheesy message in *his* name?

He glanced quickly at Macy, who watched with unconcealed anticipation for his reaction.

It had to be Gus sticking his nose in where it didn't belong, not taking no for an answer. He'd find out for sure when he tracked Bernie down but, in the meantime, how was he going to get out of this without the truth of the mayor's thoughtless actions humiliating and hurting Macy?

Where have you been all my life?

A knot in Macy's stomach tightened the longer Jake struggled to put into words the intent of the flowers and note. How had she not realized they'd only been meant as a lighthearted thank you for stepping in to help with the fund-raiser?

She swallowed down a feeling that she refused to admit was disappointment and focused on her rising embarrassment over the way she'd put him on the spot. She should have recognized sending flowers and mushy messages for romantic reasons was unlike Jake. It most certainly was at odds with where their own relationship currently stood. Her teasing had clearly made him uncomfortable.

A wave of heat washing through her, she fixed a smile in place and plucked the card from the hands of a startled Jake. Then she tucked it back in with the foliage. She could fix this—she just had to let him know she understood.

"It was sweet of you to send me a thank-you gift

on behalf of Canyon Springs but, truly, I'm more than happy to help with the fund-raiser."

By the blank look on his face, she could tell his mind was scrambling, working overtime to digest the words releasing him from the obligation to explain the flowers.

"You're welcome." Shifting his weight, he glanced uneasily at the floral arrangement, not contradicting her assessment. A flash of irritation bolted through her. If he wanted to thank her, why didn't he simply say thank you in the note? He was an attorney. He understood the power of words and their nuances. Why the lovely lady comment and a classic—and misleading—pickup line?

But then again, this was Jake.

Please, Lord, let him be so relieved at not having to embarrass us both with an explanation that he'll forget about my silly assumptions. What an idiot she'd been, allowing the flowers to goad her into practically flirting with him the moment he'd walked in the door.

"We appreciate your help." With an ill-at-ease glance in her direction, he moved again toward the door, hardly able to get away from her fast enough. "Have a good rest of your evening, Macy."

"You, too."

But he'd only gotten a few doors down the hallway when she stepped to the threshold and called out behind him. "Don't forget the recipe."

Chapter Nine

"**W**hat did you think you were doing permitting someone to send flowers to Macy Colston in my name?" He hadn't called Bernie over the weekend, deciding a face-to-face conversation Monday morning would get his point across better.

The plump, salt-and-pepper-haired florist smiled as she tucked a satin bow spike into a milky white vase of pink carnations and baby's breath.

"No need to thank me. You'd have done it yourself if you'd have thought of it. I know you're a busy man, so I did the thinking for you."

"It was *your* idea to send them?"

The florist shrugged. "Sort of."

"Bernie, I have a business relationship with Ms. Colston. The flowers and that…that 'where have you been all my life' made things extremely awkward between us."

"She didn't like them?" Her pencil-thin brows tented.

He…wasn't sure. She'd seemed pleased enough at

first. That is, until he wavered in his response. Then things got uncomfortable. Had she thought the flowers signaled something more on his part? Was that the question that seemed to hang in the air between them when he'd arrived? Surely she didn't think anything had changed between them.

"It wasn't that she didn't like them, it was—"

A smile again lit Bernie's round face. "You can't go wrong with flowers. Most women love them and sincere compliments. I thought the 'lovely lady' made a nice touch, didn't you?"

She gave the vase a spin to check it from all angles and he reached out to halt it. "I know you meant well, but it was inappropriate. Please don't do it again."

Looking him in the eye, she shook her head as if dealing with a headstrong child. "I'm only trying to help, Jake. Doing my part for Canyon Springs. And for *you*."

"What are you talking about? What part?"

She straightened the bow. "You know, I'm helping you win Macy's heart."

What? "Bernie, I'm not trying to win her heart."

"That's not what Gus—" Her lips clamped shut.

"What did Gus say?" He could almost guess without Bernie saying another word.

"Nothing." She carried the vase to a glass-fronted cooling unit, Jake right behind her.

"Tell me."

A knowing smile played on her lips. "I told him it was a bad idea when I thought you were just making a big sacrifice on the part of our town. But after I met her, I realized Gus must have known you were interested in courting her for real."

His ears warmed. His sister had once told him they turned pink when he was embarrassed. Did anyone else notice besides a bratty little sister?

"There is no courtship."

"Of course there is." She looked at him as if he were a simpleton.

"There isn't."

Why was he having this discussion about his personal life with a fellow council member?

She shook her finger at him, eyes narrowing. "Don't lead her on, Jake. She's a sweet girl who doesn't deserve that, not to mention that it could hurt the town. Hurt you in particular, if you want to get the support of the council. I'm hearing your name bandied about as a replacement for the vice mayor. That's a coup for a still-green councilman. But if you go breaking that girl's heart…"

She clucked her tongue.

"I'm not—"

The bell above the door jingled and Jake swung around to see Cate Landreth entering as she chatted away on her cell phone. He gave Bernie a warning look.

Cate covered the mouthpiece, her eyes full of mischief. "Ordering flowers for a special someone, Jake?"

A smothering sensation enveloping him, he nevertheless rallied a smile. "No. I. Am. Not. Have a good day, Bernie. You too, Cate."

Desperate to give Gus some straight talk, he slipped past the redhead and out onto Main Street— and plowed right into former city councilman Reuben Falkner.

Jake stepped back from the stocky gentleman with a crew cut. "Sorry, Mr. Falkner."

The former marine, now in his late sixties, did his best to stare Jake down. "You'd better be looking where you're going, young man. Get your head out of the clouds."

Jake nodded, jaw clenched. He wasn't up to dealing with Reuben this morning. He had to get over to the mayor's office to lay down the law before this courting Macy thing got out of hand. It had the potential to be disastrous on every level. He stepped around Reuben.

"You're aware, I assume, that you wouldn't be sitting in a council seat if it weren't for my granddaughter pulling out before the election."

The older man's low, mocking words halted him.

When Reuben's term neared its end last year, he'd prepared to leave office under the assumption Lindi would step into his vacancy to continue the family tradition. It was only by an unexpected twist that for the first time in decades the Falkner clan didn't have a representative on the city council.

Reluctantly, Jake turned toward him. This wasn't

the first time the disgruntled grandfather had brought this "fluke" to his attention.

"Nevertheless, I am on the council," he said firmly, keeping his tone and expression benign. He wasn't in any mood to be intimidated, but nevertheless refrained from pointing out that had Reuben's granddaughter stayed in town, her past mistakes and subsequent cover-up would have impacted the election results, as well.

Reuben grunted, his expression suddenly keen. "So what are they going to do with your grandfather's old place anyway? Prime piece of property, that one. The city could use the revenue from its sale."

Reuben probably sensed his frustration with seeing it slip out of the family's control. Could he want to get his hands on it himself? Jake met his belligerent gaze. "A decision hasn't been made yet."

"I hear you're stonewalling," Reuben said, then tipped his glasses down on his nose to gaze over the top of them. "I think you're letting your own attachment to it sway your thinking to the detriment of the community. I hear most of the council is ready to sell, but you're holding up the show with your legal tactics."

Jake managed another smile, knowing Reuben was trying to get him to do or say something that could be used against him. "No legal tactics at all. I'm making sure everything is taken care of according to the city's rules and regs, that we follow our own procedures."

Reuben's mouth curled downward, then with a

snort of disdain, he headed off to annoy another un-
suspecting victim.

Jake stood for a moment, staring after him, uncom-
fortably aware Cate probably had her nose pressed
to the florist shop window, ears straining to catch a
word or two. Reuben and Granddad had never gotten
along. No public feuds but always at loggerheads on
some point or other. Uninterested in politics, Granddad never held an elected office, but he'd been influential in a way Reuben could never hope to be.

Surprisingly, one point where Jake and Reuben
agreed was on the importance of the town retaining
its rustic mountain flavor with locally owned businesses. Reuben must have really been reaching for a
way to exasperate Jake to accuse him of holding the
town back from taking the first offer on the property. Though the cantankerous old man would never
admit it, Jake was sure Reuben knew about his commitment to boosting the local economy in ways that
would be in character with what the town stood for.

Speaking of which, he still needed to have a talk
with Gus about the kind of fake courtship the town
did *not* stand for. With a grimace, he again turned toward the mayor's office. Then he halted. Macy stood
under an awning not a dozen feet away, her intent
gaze trained on him.

"Trouble in paradise, Jake?" A teasing curve surfaced on her pretty mouth, but he recognized the look
in her eyes. Macy was on the prowl for a news story.
How much had she overheard?

"Good morning, Macy." Pasting on a smile, he took her arm and drew her farther down the street, away from the florist shop's window.

Macy glanced over his shoulder. "That was Reuben Falkner, wasn't it? A former councilman. I met him the first day I arrived."

"That was, indeed, Mr. Falkner."

She tossed back her golden hair and focused on Jake. "What property is he talking about that your grandfather gave the town? Is that the same one Sharon referred to yesterday? You don't want it to be sold?"

What could he say, without being confrontational, to convince her the issue was of no consequence and certainly not anything she'd wish to feature in an online post? A private conflict between him and a former council member might get her attention, but it wasn't anything he cared to see elaborated on in her blog.

"It's a plot of land with a small house and the city is trying to determine how to best dispose of it."

"Reuben made it sound as if you're the sole barrier to releasing it for sale."

"Not hardly." He wasn't fabricating. Larry, especially, had his doubts.

"His granddaughter ran against you last year? Is that what he said? Then she pulled out of the race?"

Why wouldn't she let this go? "She and her family had personal issues to take care of and relocated to Phoenix."

"So you won?"

"I'd have won anyway."

Macy made an apologetic grimace. "Oh, I didn't mean to imply you wouldn't have."

"No offense taken. So what are you doing out and about on a Monday morning? You looked as if you were waiting for someone."

For a moment he didn't think she'd allow herself to be diverted. A fleeting frown creased her forehead, then she motioned across the street to the second story city council office.

"Your mayor is supposed to give me an insider's tour of the town."

If Gus was tied up with Macy, there'd be no chance to lodge his objections to the older man's interference in his personal life—not just with the flowers, but with other things, as well. In thinking back over the past few days, he should have seen the signs his friend was up to something. Why else would Larry have insisted he'd loan him an extra mountain bike if Gus hadn't put a bug in his ear?

"Make sure he takes you to the lake and fills you in on the history of Canyon Springs's early years. That might provide a few posts for your blog."

"I'll remind him."

The phone in her purse played a muffled tune. She gave him an apologetic glance and pulled it out to check caller ID. "It's Gus."

Jake nodded for her to take the call and stepped slightly away, providing at least the illusion of privacy. He should probably take off and not risk her refocusing on the city council and his granddad's property.

"Hello, Gus. Oh, I'm sorry to hear that." She paused, and Jake strained to hear her next words. Was Gus reneging on his promised tour? "Thank you, but please don't go to any trouble. Okay. Okay. I'll stay put."

She glanced at Jake as she put away her phone. "Change in plans. He's sending a substitute tour guide and says I'm to stay right where I am."

"That's a shame, I—"

Jake's phone vibrated and he pulled it from the clip on his belt. Gus. With a sinking feeling he excused himself and stepped away from Macy to take the call.

"What's up?"

"I promised our esteemed visitor the grand tour of town today," Gus said jovially and Jake gritted his teeth, knowing what was coming next. "I can't fulfill my obligations and I'm afraid my bowing out is disrupting her schedule."

"I see."

"So I'm handing the reins over to you, my friend. I know I can count on you to make the day memorable. For both of you."

Acutely aware of Macy's presence, Jake's mind raced as he discreetly searched the second story windows across the street. Thank goodness Macy was occupied hunting for something in her purse.

Maybe he was being paranoid, but...nope, he

wasn't. There was Gus, peeping out from a city council chamber window. He grinned when he realized Jake had spied him.

"You're looking especially sharp this morning, Mr. Talford. I imagine Macy thinks so, too. Have a great day." The phone went dead and Gus gave him a quick wave before stepping back into the shadows.

Resigned, Jake clipped the phone to his belt. If he could steer her clear of council business, it might not be a half-bad idea to spend more time with Macy. She could hardly be pumping townspeople for story ideas if he stayed glued to her side. Maybe he could find out what she had brewing for the blog and head off anything he deemed inappropriate.

"Is everything okay?" Macy zipped up her purse and secured the strap over her shoulder.

"That depends on how you feel about having me for a guide."

The corners of her mouth turned downward. "That was Gus, wasn't it? I'm sorry."

He gave a courtly bow. "I'm at your service, Ms. Colston."

She laughed, but shook her head. "Thank you, Jake, but I can't impose on you. I'm sure you have other plans for the morning."

Only to strangle Gus.

"Nothing pressing whatsoever."

"It's awkward, isn't it?" She lowered her voice. "You know, with no one knowing we knew each other before."

"It might be more awkward if they did." How would he explain to the council his objections to Macy's visit if they knew they shared a past? They'd wonder why he hadn't said anything before and want an explanation. Details. "But if *you* prefer not to be seen around town with *me,* I understand."

She stepped forward to place her hand on his arm. "You know it's not that. I don't want to impose."

"You're not imposing." Didn't the word imply being a nuisance? A burden? Macy had been a lot of things that had thrown his world into a tailspin, but she'd never been that. "Be aware, though, you may not get the in-depth expedition Gus could offer. I am, after all, an adopted son of the community. But I've been brushing up on local history in recent weeks and imagine I can hold my own."

She quirked a smile. "I'm willing to take my chances if you are."

Gazing down at her upturned face, he was suddenly more than willing.

Chapter Ten

Jake ducked under the tall metal slide at the elementary school playground and pointed down low on its underside. "And if you look closely there, you'll see where I scratched my name with a rock."

Macy peeked under the slide then quickly drew back, acutely aware of Jake's too-close proximity. Not that she minded being a hairbreadth away from him, but she feared reawakening the awkwardness they'd shared in the earlier hours of their tour. Residual fallout from the flower episode?

He'd already taken her to Casey Lake and to the remains of the first structure in what later became Canyon Springs. Only an overgrown, crumbling foundation with a stone fireplace stood sentinel, a reminder of the photo of Orian and Harva Bigelow she'd found during her first day at the museum. Jake's input combined with Ava's facts fleshed out the story in her mind. She'd snapped a few pictures before they'd moved on to their next stop.

"I never expected you'd be the type to desecrate public property, Mr. Councilman." Macy couldn't help but cut him a challenging look.

"Hey, now, I was in second grade. Give me a break." His fingers traced the nearly invisible letters. Then he popped out from under the slide, too, and grinned down at her. "Are you thinking I had the makings of a street hood or mobster or something?"

"Never."

His gaze held hers as if judging her sincerity, then he looked away.

Years ago, Jake hadn't shared a lot about his past and she'd never given it much thought back then. Had he not wanted to talk about it or had the then twenty-nine-year-old recognized the barely-into-her-twenties coed was caught up in her own little world? Looking back, it was a wonder he'd paid her any attention at all.

"You lived here for how long?" she prompted, hoping he'd tell her more now.

He didn't respond immediately, as if weighing the wisdom of wading too deeply into the past. "A year. When Mom took us back to her hometown after the divorce, she promised me and my sister we'd stay here forever. We thought this place was better than Disneyland, with Grandma and Granddad an added bonus."

"But you didn't stay."

"No."

He moved around to the front of the slide and

gazed up at the rolling surface glinting in the sun, a handsome figure whose strong, rugged profile reflected the inner man he'd grown up to be. A divorce at that young age couldn't have been easy on him.

"That's when you moved back to Phoenix."

"Right. It didn't take Mom long to realize she couldn't provide for us as a housekeeper at Kit's. I later learned child support checks were few and far between and there wasn't any place within driving distance to put her degree in microbiology to good use. Sad to say, that's a drawback to little towns."

"Your grandparents couldn't help out?"

He glanced back at her, a light breeze ruffling his hair. "Oh, they offered to. In fact, we lived with them the year I was in school here. But they'd raised an independent daughter who packed us up and headed back to the Valley."

"That's a shame. A child growing up in Canyon Springs would have so many advantages." Advantages she herself, being raised in St. Louis, certainly hadn't had.

"I later overheard Mom telling Grandma," he continued, his eyes focusing on something in the distance, "that Dad had pressured her to come back to Phoenix so he could spend more time with his kids. Mom thought it was important to keep us in a relationship with him, but it turned out to be a joke."

"How come?" she whispered, not wanting to disrupt his thoughts.

Jake gripped the edge of the slide. "It seems he'd

landed a new job with a small, family-friendly company. In the interviews, he'd portrayed himself as the consummate family man. So he needed to make good on that image. But as with many of Dad's employment ventures, it was short-lived and his attention to his offspring soon waned, as well."

"I had no idea your father wasn't in the picture."

He lifted his shoulders in a shrug. "He moved out of state not long after that. I hear from him once in a while. But it's awkward. Two strangers."

"Did your mother remarry? Did you have a stepfather?" She hated to think of Jake growing up without the love and affection of a father.

"That was an 'interesting' experience, too." Jake's mouth twisted into a mocking half smile as he walked along the slide toward the ladder, his hand trailing the curved steel edge and the sun dappling through the pines onto his broad shoulders. "When Barry, my stepdad, and Mom first tied the knot, he made all sorts of noises about me being his new son. About spending man time together. We played baseball and video games, shot baskets in the driveway and went to a couple of Phoenix Suns games. I was in fifth grade by then and in hog heaven."

"I'm glad. You deserved a real dad." Someone who cared about him. Invested time in him.

"Unfortunately..." He smacked the edge of the slide with the heel of his hand, his expression hard. "It only lasted a couple of years until his and mom's first born arrived on the scene. A boy. A few months later he sat me down to say he had more pressing obligations to attend to with the tiny newcomer. 'No hard feelings, but you already have a dad.'"

A tiny sound escaped Macy's throat. "How cruel."

"I'd sure never do that to a little kid." He pushed away from the slide, bringing himself back to the present. "But is it any wonder I gravitated to my granddad as a role model?"

"I'm sorry, Jake."

His brows abruptly lowered as if suddenly realizing he'd been reminiscing aloud. "You're not going to put any of this in your blog are you?"

He shouldn't have asked that. He could see the hurt plainly written in her eyes, but it was too late to take back the words.

"No, Jake," she said quietly, the easy rapport between them evaporating. "I won't put any of this in my blog."

"I'm sorry, Macy, I didn't—"

"I know you have little reason to trust me, but things would be more comfortable between us if you'd accept that I'm not out to exploit you or your town." She stepped closer, a sadness lingering in her expression. "I'm here to promote it, to bring it alive for my readers who long for a simpler way of life. Readers who dream of neighbors they can count on and who dream of friendships that last a lifetime."

"You're doing a nice job so far." But by the downward curve of her mouth, she wasn't convinced he genuinely thought so. The "so far" he'd unthinkingly tacked on implied he expected her to change tactics tomorrow. To lure him in, then spring something on him. "Look, Macy—"

"No, you look, Jake." Her brow furrowed. "Something like eighty percent of Americans live in urban areas. People dream of having what you have here. I do my best to portray the rural towns I visit so my readers can live in them vicariously in some respects. I try to share a place for them to start the day on a positive note or come home to at the end of a stressful day. There's no hidden agenda. Can you not understand that?"

She abruptly turned her back on him and marched stiffly toward his SUV parked a short distance away.

Was he letting one point in time color his perceptions of her? Making assumptions that were no longer true? He caught up with her in a few easy strides just as she reached his vehicle.

"That's what brought me here," he admitted, gazing at the bowed head that stubbornly refused to look up at him. "The people. Life on a smaller scale. A place where church choir presentations and high school football games are every bit as thrilling as a big name rock concert or professional sports."

When she didn't respond, he opened the door and she silently slipped inside. Gritting his teeth, he carefully shut the door. They were strangers, yet that morning they'd found themselves falling into old familiar patterns. Teasing. Catching each other's eye. Long-forgotten jokes resurfaced. Once he'd almost reached for her hand before bringing himself up short. Then, just like now, they'd abruptly, self-consciously, remembered they weren't a young couple exploring rural Missouri together on a Sunday afternoon anymore. They were two people with a past whose present had no hope but to cross only briefly.

Striding around the front of the vehicle, conscious of her gaze on him through the windshield, he then climbed in beside her and fastened his seat belt. He rammed the key into the ignition.

"It's all your fault, you know." Her words came softly, but nevertheless held an accusing edge.

Hackles rising, he shot a look in her direction, but she was staring out the side window. "What's all my fault?"

He hadn't been the one to betray a confidence.

"The blog." She turned her attention to her hands folded in her lap. "You introduced me to the small-town treasures surrounding us. Seeing them through your eyes made them like hidden jewels."

With considerable effort, he tamped down his confusion. "You seemed to enjoy exploring them."

"I did. The spring of my senior year I couldn't help but think about starting a blog to capture the flavor of the wonderful places we'd visited."

Maybe he'd inspired her blog, but at the same time she'd been researching a story that would rip his world apart. Betray his trust. He held his tongue now, though, mindful that they'd shared a mostly enjoyable morning despite tiptoeing around their shared past.

"Six years is a long time to keep at a blog." He rested his hands on the steering wheel, willing her to look at him.

"It is."

"Tell me more about how you got this far with it."

To his relief, after a moment she offered him a quick glance accompanied by a half smile. It was probably pretty obvious he was following her lead to smooth things over.

She settled back in the leather bucket seat, clasped her seat belt, then gave a little sigh. Relief? Resignation?

"After graduation—" she tactfully censored mention of their parting ways "—I started out as a reporter for a Columbia paper. Then on weekends I'd return to the places we'd visited and blog about them."

"Boonville. Westphalia. Rocheport. You always loved their history." Had she thought about him when she went back to the towns they'd explored? Did she miss him at her side? He couldn't imagine bringing himself to visit them again without her, so that was a confirming sign she hadn't felt about him the way he'd felt about her.

"And Hermann. Arrow Rock. Centralia. Amazingly, others enjoyed learning about the towns, too, and the blog gathered a loyal regional following.

When the *St. Louis Post-Dispatch* did a feature article on it, the blog's popularity expanded rapidly."

"Then towns started inviting you to come visit."

With a satisfied laugh, she finally really looked at him. "At their expense, unbelievably, in exchange for featuring their communities in my blog."

"Now you receive invitations from all over."

She nodded. "It really took off three years ago when my sister landed me a major sponsor and started overseeing publicity."

"Your folks are good with it?" It was quite a switch from investigative reporting. Her mom, a former journalist herself, had always been at Macy to keep up her grades, to be more assertive in her dealings with others, more aggressive in her reporting. He'd overheard tense phone conversations between mother and daughter more than he cared to, but learned the hard way to keep out of it.

Not unexpectedly, Macy's lips tightened. "Why wouldn't they be?"

He shrugged, instinctively backing off. It didn't look like much had changed in that department. "So where do you go from here? What's in your future?"

She leaned slightly toward him, her lips softening and excitement lighting her eyes. "My sponsor wants to approach a specialty cable network about a pilot for a television program."

He raised his brows. "Wow."

"Pretty cool, huh?"

"What kind of show?"

Her smile broadened. "I'd continue doing what I'm doing now, exploring small towns. Except it would be filmed."

She'd be in a reality show where a camera crew followed her around? It was impressive if you were inclined to go that route, but it didn't sound fun to him. It was hard enough being in the public eye in his community service role, let alone being filmed every time you scratched your nose. He'd have to get used to that, though, if things progressed toward the capitol steps.

She laughed and poked him in the arm. "Get that look off your face, Jake Talford. It wouldn't be one of those celebrity deals where I'm on camera 24-7 and pouring out my inner angst. I picture it as more like those shows food critics do, where they travel around and visit different restaurants. I'm guessing portions of my visits would be filmed, then edited to a more compact, storylike form."

"So you'd be recorded doing things similar to our tour of town today?" He shuddered inwardly at the thought.

"Right. Meeting locals. Learning about their history, their professions, their families."

Encouraging people to spill their guts in front of a camera? She'd be good at that. Look at what she'd effortlessly gotten him to reveal about himself this morning. "That would be a lot of traveling."

She tilted her head thoughtfully. "Possibly. Definitely more intense than my blog schedule is now. I think those programs do a lot of filming in a short period of time, maybe a month or two several times a year, then break them up into individual broadcasts."

"Would you spend two to four weeks in each town as you do now?"

"I suppose it depends on whether each segment is a stand-alone or more of a serial. If I'm popping from place to place each week, I'm not sure how I could get to know a town well enough to deliver in a filmed version what I'm able to deliver on the blog. But I'll cross that bridge when I come to it." A shadow flitted briefly through her eyes, but he picked up on it. "My family assures me it's the right move."

"You're not sure yourself?"

Macy shook back her hair as if reinforcing her own confidence. "My mom and sister have been helping me work toward this for years. And yes, it's a big step that will present new challenges."

He could almost feel the protective hackles rising on his neck. "Are they pressuring you?"

"Opportunities like this are fleeting, Jake." Her expression flattened to a matter-of-fact look. "You may not remember, but I come from a family of over-achievers. A dad who is the CEO of a big insurance company, a brother who's a Wall Street executive and two sisters who are skyrocketing in their chosen fields."

He hadn't forgotten. Nor had he forgotten the mother who'd failed to attain her own career goals and lived vicariously through her youngest daughter.

"And me?" Macy gave a self-deprecating laugh. "I'm the black sheep of the family. A lowly professional blogger."

"Don't say it like that, Macy." He leaned over to cover her small, delicate hands with his. He sensed her breath catch as their gazes locked. "Don't discount your own achievements."

She nibbled at her lower lip.

"But it would be sweet, wouldn't it?" Her eyes appealed for understanding. "To have a television program? That would boost me in the family ratings for sure."

"That's why you're pursuing this? To earn your family's approval? Whose dream is this—yours or your mother's?"

She pulled her hands free and pinned him with a warning look. "You're an attorney, Jake. Don't play amateur psychologist. I'm doing this because I want to. Me, myself and I. God leads and I follow."

He took the hint and grimly sat back in his seat, started the engine and put the SUV in gear.

But he wasn't buying it.

Chapter Eleven

❧

"I sent you an email," Ava said Wednesday night. "Info your readers may enjoy about the family who established Kit's Lodge."

"Thank you." Looking away from the tableau in front of her—laptop, a fruit plate beside it and a single daisy in a vase gracing the table—Macy glanced around the almost-vacant premises of Hector's High Country Steakhouse. Only a piped-in country and western beat in the background and a parquet dance floor in the middle of the raftered room suggested the restaurant would be packed during the summer season.

The scheduled switch to her new abode at Nancy's Bed and Breakfast had taken place that afternoon, but she'd been restless, unable to settle down and work despite her charming surroundings. With the clock ticking steadily toward tomorrow's 12 a.m. post time, she'd commandeered a secluded corner at a nearby eatery to hammer out her blog. Or at least that had been the plan.

"You're a lifesaver, Ava. I've been racking my brain to come up with a topic for tomorrow."

"What's up? You're always full of ideas. You even write them up days in advance."

"I know." She stared at the blank screen, relieved to have a distraction from thoughts of her recent conversation with Jake. "Maybe I'm feeling a little pressured."

"From your family, I assume."

"My sponsor, too."

And Jake. She'd given him the high road version of the purpose of *Hometowns With Heart* the other day. Would her plans for the future compromise that?

"Be true to yourself, Macy, and to God." Ava clucked her tongue. "You can't go wrong that way."

"I suppose not."

"So, are you ready for an update on that Dexter Smith fellow?" Ava's playful tone suggested her answer should be yes. "I'm not finding anything on your Canyon Springs Dexter, but out of curiosity I pursued the other Dexter, the one who died in 1941. I confirmed he did die at Pearl Harbor and he was raised in an orphanage outside of Chicago."

"That's sad." She couldn't imagine a little kid having no family to raise him, or to mourn him after he died in service to his country. Macy glanced at the blossoms of the daisy on her table. Delicate, fragile.

Like life. "Do you think he could be my Dexter's uncle? Cousin?"

"No, I'm afraid not. This Dexter didn't appear to have had any living family by the time of his death." Macy could hear Ava clicking away at her keyboard. "The strange thing is they both have the same birthday."

"As in month and day you mean?"

Ava made a humming noise. "Month, day—and year. It's odd, to say the least. I know this guy who died years ago isn't your Dexter, but now the pair of them have aroused my curiosity."

"I can see why. I wonder—" Her journalist's mind raced with possible explanations. Maybe a typographical error that wasn't corrected? That wasn't uncommon back then.

"It could be a coincidence," Ava reminded her. "You do see a lot of those when you do genealogical research. More than you'd think. I couldn't find much on the background of your Dexter, but I did find an archived article in the hometown paper of my Pearl Harbor Dexter with a picture of him and another orphan buddy, Tommy O'Donner, when they joined the navy in 1940. They're fresh-faced teenagers in the photo, eager to get out on their own and serve their country."

"It's bittersweet, isn't it, to look back from our perspective and know what happens to him the following year." Just as who would ever have guessed that by the summer after she and Jake met their relationship would end so disastrously?

"In genealogy you often get attached to the people you research, feel their hopes, dreams, disappointments. I look at these two young men, so handsome in what I imagine were the best clothes they owned, as they set out for basic training. They didn't have a clue how tragically their friendship would end."

"Do you know what happened to the other guy? Tommy? Was he at Pearl Harbor, too?"

"I'll need to do more research. Records in these small-town papers haven't been indexed, so you can't just type in a name or date and pull up a match. It's very manual. Lots of reading."

"Labor intensive."

"Right. I won't spend too much time on this guy because I know you need facts on the other names you've given me."

"Maybe you can get back to him next month and satisfy your curiosity. Mine, too."

She'd barely shut off her phone when a young waiter appeared at her table. Justin, the restaurant owner's son, reached for her water glass, almost knocking it over, then filled it precariously to the brim.

He stepped back, fidgeting with the pitcher's handle. "Miss Colston?"

"Yes?" Was he going to ask her for an autograph? She still couldn't get used to people doing that.

"I hate to impose." He glanced toward the front of

the restaurant where his father stood chatting with someone in the shadows of the entry. "I know you wanted a quiet place to work. But do you mind if I seat someone else with you?"

She winced. She'd barely started her dinner and the laptop's cursor blinked accusingly on the still-blank screen. Even with the timely arrival of Ava's information, she had more than a couple of hours of work ahead of her. She wasn't a speedy writer, and formatting, scheduling and selecting suitable digital photos could be time consuming.

"They can't be seated elsewhere?" She looked pointedly at the handful of tables presently occupied. The rest were empty. Had someone seen her and requested to join her? The dim light of the steakhouse didn't enlighten her as to who the owner was conversing with.

Justin's Adam's apple bobbed. "Dad says we might get a rush from a post-theater crowd. They could show up any minute."

"Maybe it would be better if I let your patron have the table." Macy logged out of her document and clicked the shutdown icon. "Would you please bring me a take-out box?"

"No!" His flush deepened and he glanced again toward the far side of the room. "I mean, we don't want to rush you off."

"You're not." She closed her laptop and mustered a smile. Poor kid, having to deliver the message on behalf of his father. "The creative juices don't seem to be flowing tonight."

"But—" The teen's head rotated between her and the front of the restaurant in an almost cartoonish fashion.

"A take-out box, please?"

"Uh…sure." He set the pitcher down with a thud, sending the water sloshing, then took off for the kitchen.

Shaking her head, Macy slid her laptop into its soft-sided case.

"Ms. Colston?"

Startled, she looked up as a beaming Hector Lopez approached—with Jake right behind him.

"I knew you wouldn't mind being seated with one of our city's finest." The statement of Jake's fellow councilman left little room for an obviously surprised Macy to argue. "I understand he's already shown you around our fair city."

Jake scowled. How'd Hector know that? They'd been to the lake, the old Bigelow place and an empty school yard. Not exactly Canyon Springs hot spots. They'd barely seen another soul on their outing, but clearly the local grapevine had struck again. Even if Hector had taken to reading Macy's blog, including Tuesday's post that featured their outing, Jake hadn't been named or photographed.

Hector motioned to him. "Jake was telling me what a fine writer you are. Right, Jake?"

Jake frowned at his friend. When he'd walked in the door of the restaurant, Hector had immediately asked him if he thought Macy was a good writer— and if he considered her pretty. What else could he have done but confirm both?

"Right. Extremely talented."

"And pretty, as well." Hector gave Macy a wink and Jake a slight push. "Sit down, sit down, before our guest gets a crick in her neck looking up at you."

Jake offered an apologetic smile, reluctant to intrude. While enjoyable for the most part, their Monday outing had ended on a strained note. "Macy?"

"Please sit down." She gestured to the purse and laptop bag on the chair beside her. "I was finishing up here."

From the looks of her barely touched plate, it didn't appear she was finishing up anything. He hesitated a moment, then pulled out the chair across from her and seated himself.

Macy reached for her purse.

"No, no, Ms. Colston, take your time. Eat your meal." Hector whipped out a menu and handed it to Jake. "Filet mignon special tonight. Mesquite grilled. Baked potato. Steamed veggies. Medium-well as usual?"

Caught off guard, he nodded and Hector snatched the oversize, laminated card out of his hands.

"Would you care for something more, as well?" Jake looked to Macy, hating to down a steak with all the trimmings while she nibbled on cold fruit.

"I'm fine, thank you. I've been consuming an extraordinary amount of calorie-laden home cooking the past week and a half and needed lighter fare this evening."

"I can vouch for Canyon Springs having the best cooks in the country," Hector said as he nodded emphatically. "Isn't that right, Jake?"

"Oh, right."

"This is a great place to raise a family, too. Top-notch schools. Active churches. Best hometown in the country with more heart than your blog has ever seen. Jake here is one of our finest examples of an upstanding resident." The older man raised a brow in his direction and Jake's ears warmed. "Isn't that right?"

What had gotten into this guy anyway? A chat with the mayor that morning assured him Gus wasn't stirring things up behind the scenes. But Don, Larry, Bernie and now Hector pushing him at Macy? It seemed too coincidental and embarrassingly obvious.

"You know I love to talk about Canyon Springs, but I'm mighty hungry." Jake rested his arm on the edge of the table and leaned forward. "Do you think you can get that grill fired up in record time?"

The restaurant's owner stared at him blankly for a moment, then a knowing gleam entered his eyes and he stepped back from the table. "I most certainly can. I'll leave you two alone."

To the rhythm of an old Brooks & Dunn tune, both sat in silence as their gazes followed the man's retreat. But when Hector disappeared behind a swinging door, they cautiously turned to catch the other's eye. Macy's shoulders shook in mirthful silence and Jake was unable to suppress a smile.

"I'm sorry, Macy. I know you're trying to work. I offered to go elsewhere but he wouldn't hear of it."

"No problem. Mr. Lopez says the tables are being conserved against the chance of a post-theater crowd."

"You believe that?"

Macy giggled. "It does sound fishy."

"What can I say? Hector got remarried on Valentine's Day this year. His first wife died when Justin was small. So I think he has matchmaking on his mind."

"So you're not really one of the finest examples of an upstanding Canyon Springs resident? That was a sales pitch?"

Jake leaned his forearms on the table and gazed at the pretty lady across from him. When he'd finished his editing for the evening, filled Abe's dog dish and headed out the door to grab a late supper, he sure hadn't anticipated a dinner companion.

Divine intervention?

"Sales pitch? I wouldn't go as far as to say that. I seem to have turned out okay."

Her eyes twinkled. "Only okay?"

Jake opened his mouth to respond, finding the banter more than appealing, similar to what they once shared, but the movements of a man seated across the room caught his attention. High school principal Ben

Cameron gave him a thumbs-up. Thankfully, Macy didn't turn in time to see his gesture of support.

Throat suddenly parched, Jake reached for the water glass on the table, then remembered it was Macy's and withdrew his hand. He motioned to her plate. "Go ahead and eat. Don't wait for me. It might be a while."

She dipped her head in acknowledgment and slid the plate in front of her, then broke off a juicy green grape from the cluster. "I've already seen posters advertising the fund-raiser. Did Paris or Sharon get hold of you about your part?"

"My part? With what I have going on right now, it had better be pretty minor."

"Emceeing."

He shook his head. "That's a job for our esteemed mayor. You're giving the keynote, though, right? What are you going to talk about?"

She popped the grape into her mouth, chewed, swallowed. Then reached for her fork. "My journalism background. Love of history. How I got started blogging."

His stomach knotted. "How can you do that without mentioning me? You claimed I had a hand in those beginnings."

Despite her assurance that nothing he'd shared while on the playground would make its way to her blog, uneasiness had resurfaced that evening before he'd fallen asleep. She'd only be here another two weeks, but could still do irrevocable harm to the town—and him—if she so chose.

The following morning he'd dreaded checking *Hometowns With Heart,* but her post sang the praises of the tour. He liked that she didn't call him by name, referring to him only as Mr. Councilman. But she couldn't say at the fundraiser that Mr. Councilman introduced her to small towns. Everyone would put two and two together.

"Relax." Her lips tucked into a smile. "I'll refer to you as a friend. That should be safe enough. You *were* a friend, weren't you?"

That and then some.

"Okay. That will work."

She stabbed a pear slice, studying him a long moment. "So how's the book coming along?"

He should have known he couldn't keep anything from her in this town. "Who told you about the book?"

She shrugged and bit into the fruit. "You'd be surprised what you can pick up at Camilla's Café without even trying. Somebody said you were writing a Canyon Springs history."

He clasped his hands on the table. "Actually, I'm only editing it. And it's not a history exactly. You know, not a sequential 'this happened and then that happened.' It's more of a series of sketches highlighting those who've made a contribution to the town. My granddad wrote the draft before he died. I'm polishing it up. Verifying facts."

Her eyes widened slightly. "That's why you came into the museum looking for Sandi last week?"

"That's right." He smiled as realization dawned in her eyes. "And *you* accused me of following you around. For a while there, I thought you'd call the police and press charges."

Flushing, she cringed. "Sorry."

"I guess we've both been a little paranoid, haven't we?"

"It's true, I confess." She speared a piece of pineapple. "But at least you knew I was coming here and could prepare yourself. I didn't have a clue you called Canyon Springs home until you loomed over my table at Kit's and your glower sent that poor teenage girl flying out of the restaurant."

"Glower?"

"Yes, glower." She waved the fork at him. "Your specialty."

He pushed back in his chair.

"You know it's true, Jake," she continued. "You're still way too serious for your own good. I thought I'd gotten you to lighten up back at Mizzou, but—"

She broke off as Justin approached the table, bringing a take-out box—so she'd definitely been planning to leave—and another water tumbler. About time. When the teen retreated, Jake lifted the pitcher and poured himself a glass, downed half of it and placed it back on the table. "Are you finished ragging on me?"

"It's for your own good." She picked at the fruit

on her plate with her fork, then set the utensil aside and focused on him. "We may not have been a match made in heaven, but I can honestly say I do care what happens to you. That I want good things for you."

He swallowed, his heart rate bumping up a notch as he lost himself in the beauty of her expressive eyes. "Same here. For you, I mean."

He'd always cared about her. Cherished her. Protected her. From the moment she'd marched boldly and flirtatiously into his life right up until the day it had all fallen apart. He still cared.

Was there a chance that the two of them had grown enough, matured enough in the years since their separation that fences could be mended? All things are possible with God, isn't that what the Good Book said? Is that why he'd hung on to that ring? Kept it tucked in the back corner of a dresser drawer?

"Nothing's truly changed, though, has it?" Her quiet gaze searched his and his spirits deflated at her blunt words. "Not the core issues. I'm still a journalist, albeit human interest stories rather than investigative reporting. And it's been obvious from the day you practically dragged me out of Kit's for a lecture that you don't trust me or think much of my career choice."

Clearing his throat, he again stretched out his hand for the water glass and took a swallow. "Maybe I was too hard on you."

The words were out of his mouth before he could take back the "maybe." Why did he tack that on? Of course he'd been too hard on her. Too stubborn. Too fearful of getting hurt again to let himself trust her, or even believe that she was deserving of trust.

Her sad smile tugged at his heart as she reached for the take-out box and slid the remainders of her fruit into it, obviously determined not to linger any longer.

"I have a feeling we'll always be too hard on each other, Jake. It's the very nature of our differences and I think God knew that and closed the door on us for a reason. But at least we seem to have called a truce. For the most part anyway, agreed?"

He nodded, a weight settling in his chest.

She rose to her feet, slinging her purse and laptop bag over her shoulder. Placing a hand over his, still gripping the tumbler, she gave it a gentle squeeze.

"You're a good man, Jake."

She picked up the take-out box, and then she was gone, her delicate, citrusy scent swirling around him, filling his senses, before fading away.

Chapter Twelve

Saturday morning Macy drank in the fresh spring air as she hurried down the street toward Camilla's Café, the lightweight wool jacket she'd picked up at a secondhand store tightly belted around her. Main Street vibrated with activity as shopkeepers swept planked porches, watered geraniums planted in big half barrels and polished display windows until they sparkled in the sunlight. Despite a nip in the air, the summer season wasn't far off. Nevertheless, her spirits didn't match the morning's promise.

For days, her thoughts had returned repeatedly to the tour Jake had given her of Canyon Springs—and to their short-lived dinner at the steakhouse. She'd more than enjoyed seeing the town through his eyes, loved listening to him share his own history here, took pleasure in talking to him. But always there had been that underlying discomfort overshadowing the present. While it waxed and waned, it inevitably re-surfaced as a reminder that, as the old saying went, there had been too much water under the bridge for them to pick up where they'd left off.

Besides, she didn't want to pick up where they'd left off. Where things ended hadn't been a happy place for either of them. Picking up where they left off would mean giving up where she was right now, on the threshold of something new, exciting, something she'd worked hard for. She'd been right to point that out to Jake a few nights ago, to make it clear they couldn't afford to gloss over the past. They'd both only end up getting hurt.

As she strode along, a shop window across the street caught her eye and a pang of hope pierced her. A wedding dress inspired by a vintage 1920s style sparkled softly in the illumination of a canister light. She couldn't draw her eyes away from it. Did God have it in his plan for her to ever marry? To be a mother? To share her life with a man she loved who loved her in return?

"Oh!" Macy stumbled back. She'd been so inwardly focused, she'd plowed right into someone.

Jake. Dressed for business in a light blue shirt, gray slacks and a well-fitted sports jacket, one look at him was enough to knock the breath out of a female of any age.

Her face burned with embarrassment as strong hands gripped her upper arms to steady her. "I'm sorry, Jake. I wasn't looking where I was going."

Dark blue eyes studied what had to be an alarmingly pink face, then he gave her an encouraging smile. "No problem. But something sure caught your attention."

Hesitant to admit the truth, she kept her eyes averted from the stunning creation across the way. But a curious Jake turned to search the street, his attention eventually falling on the tiny Sew-In-Love shop, where the sole mannequin all but waltzed before their eyes in ankle-length white lace.

He glanced back at her uncertainly.

"That would look sweet on you, Macy." Gus Gustoffsen, who'd appeared out of nowhere, gave her a conspiratorial wink. "You'll make a beautiful bride. If that one doesn't suit you, I'm sure Neva and Norma would be more than happy to sew up anything you'd like."

Jake quickly released her arms and she stepped back, attempting to regain her composure. "I'm not in need of a wedding dress, Mr. Mayor, but I fully intend to interview the owners for my blog."

Gus straightened his bolo tie. "Come now, how could a woman as beautiful and charming as you not be in need of a wedding dress?"

Jake gave Gus a dirty look, as if reminding him not to bring attention to a woman's unwed status. A quick mental calculation would clue him in that she wasn't but a couple of years from the infamous thirty mark.

"I'm not denying he's nailed the 'beautiful' and 'charming' part, Macy," Jake asserted, and her heart skittered at the sincerity in his eyes. "But Gus is giving you one of his canned promotional spins. He can't take a breath but what a persuasive tactic to buy locally comes out of his mouth."

Macy laughed, hoping the expression in her own eyes signaled awareness of—and gratefulness for—his intervention. Jake had always been sensitive to people putting others on the spot. She'd forgotten that about him, just as she'd forgotten how the shade of his shirt could intensify the blue of his eyes.

"I don't think of them as canned." Gus sucked in his cheeks, his lower lip protruding. "That implies insincerity when I sincerely believe we have the most creative businesses in the state right here in Canyon Springs."

Jake dipped his head in agreement. "I won't argue with that."

"And although Macy's only been in town two weeks," Gus continued, "Albert Keene says the chamber's website traffic has increased tenfold. So keep up the good work, Macy."

The mayor glanced at his watch before nodding a farewell and turning away to continue down the street. Then he paused to look back over his shoulder. "You, too, Jake."

She glanced curiously at her rescuer, but he didn't comment on the mayor's parting words, so she chose to ignore them, as well. "Thanks for redirecting Gus's line of conversation."

"No problem." Jake raked a hand through his hair.

"Someone's marital status is nobody's business but their own and God's. It's not open for public debate."

She should have known Jake would understand. "In my travels for the blog, I do occasionally find myself under the microscope about why I'm not married."

That was an understatement. She'd been accused by more than one man who'd taken a fancy to her of deliberately establishing a nonstop travel schedule so she could keep relationships shallow, not have to put anyone else first. The words had stung.

"But I have to admit," she added, "Canyon Springs takes more than a passing interest."

"Our unmarried state isn't out of the ordinary. After all, isn't almost half the adult population in this country single?"

"I think I've heard statistics along those lines."

"So where are you headed today?"

Why should it disappoint that he hadn't checked her schedule? "To the Warehouse for a few hours. Then to Singing Rock Cabin Resort. I'm continuing my miniseries about the three couples who got married last winter. This will be the perfect opportunity to visit with Olivia and Rob McGuire."

"Do they know you're writing about them?"

She tapped her foot, but managed a smile. He was worse than a dog with a favorite bone when he got something into his head. "I asked them and they were fine with it—as were the other two couples. They said they want to do their part to promote their favorite town."

"Be careful what you share with the public."

That sounded almost as if he knew at least one of them had things in their past they might not want broadcast to a wider audience. But she wasn't here to embarrass anyone or to dig up dirt, although her main sponsor *was* increasingly uneasy about when they'd see "some action." Macy's search for a suitable breakout story had been fruitless thus far.

"I'm careful. Discreet. I ask permission." But that hadn't always been the case and they both knew it.

"I'm not going to harangue you, Mace. Just a gentle reminder."

"Point taken." She glanced down the street, then back at Jake. "I'm stopping by Camilla's to pick up a bagel and coffee to tide me over until lunchtime. Would you care to join me?"

There was that look again. The same one from the night when the flowers had been delivered and she could tell his brain was working overtime dissecting her words, debating his options, coming to a conclusion.

Her throat tightened. "Don't sweat it. It was only a suggestion."

"I'm trying to remember what's on my calendar."

She didn't point out he had only to log on to it via his phone to settle the issue. "We probably don't have a whole lot to talk about anyway. Just old times, and you can't live in the past."

"No, I guess we can't." His gaze held hers.

She stepped back. "Well, it's been good running into you, Jake. Literally."

His smile held a melancholy that unexpectedly pulled at her heart. If God wanted them to work things out, wouldn't He have done it back then? It would be foolish to attempt to revive a relationship with her in town barely two more weeks. She had places to go and blogs—or possibly books—to write, maybe a TV pilot to film. He had clients and a town to protect and, very likely, eventually a large constituency to serve. Besides, how could she hope to regain his trust? She'd apologized; what more could she do?

But now, looking into his almost wistful eyes…

Jake gave a brisk nod. "See you at the fund-raiser then."

A whole week without seeing Jake? She bit back the words of protest that rose to her lips. "Take care," she said instead.

She turned away but had only taken a few steps when he caught her arm and drew her to a halt. She whirled toward him expectantly, hoping and praying—for what? That he'd confess his undying love for her? Ask her forgiveness for being so unbending? But occupied with fishing around in his jacket pocket, he wasn't even looking at her. After a moment, he produced a folded index card and held it out.

"I forgot to give you this."

Curious, she reached for it.

"The recipe," he clarified. "The slow-cooker roast."

"Oh, yes, thank you." She gripped the card. "Hopefully this will keep me out of hot water."

"Should do the trick."

They stood for a moment longer, then Jake lifted his hand in farewell and she turned to walk briskly across the street toward Camilla's. Once on the other side, she couldn't resist looking back, expecting to see him striding down the walkway toward his office.

But instead, he stood riveted to the ground where she'd left him, staring after her. Their gazes again held and an invisible grip tightened around her heart.

Stop chasing butterflies. He's not for you and you know it.

She waved a final goodbye, then hurried into Camilla's Café.

Jake scrolled down through Macy's blog for at least the twentieth time early the following Friday evening. He'd taken the afternoon off to diligently edit the electronic version of Granddad's history book. But almost like a kid lured to complete a task by the promise of a candy bar, he'd returned to the blog as a reward each time he finished a handful of pages.

He hadn't spoken with Macy in a week, although he'd seen her at church on Sunday, surrounded by her growing fan club. But he'd faithfully checked her *Hometowns With Heart* daily and found himself captivated not only by her photogenic smile but by her words on the screen. She *was* a good writer, painting Canyon Springs with realism, humor and affection.

As intended, she'd interviewed Norma and Neva at the custom-design clothing shop. The post featured the two talented seamstresses at work, as well as photos of Macy hamming it up in their creations, including the dress she'd obviously admired. It was that image he'd returned to each time he took a break.

Gus was right. She'd make a beautiful bride.

Heavy hearted, he shut down his computer, then strode to the living room, where he snagged his suit jacket off the back of the rocking chair. He paused to gaze at his surroundings. A rock fireplace. Soaring wood-paneled ceiling. A huge expanse of windows overlooking the oversize, ponderosa pine-studded lot.

He'd bought this place within three months of relocating to Canyon Springs, turning down Granddad's offer on the two-bedroom house and land parcel that was now in jeopardy of being sold to the highest bidder. Had he known he'd still be single six years later, he'd have certainly decided otherwise. But after the breakup with Macy, buying a four-bedroom family home seemed a step of faith, something he needed to do to illustrate his continuing intent to believe God answered prayer and would lead him to the perfect wife.

But a Mrs. Right hadn't yet shown up.

"Well, Abe," he said to the little beagle which had followed him into the spacious room. "You win some, you lose some."

Hopefully, though, even if he'd washed out in the love life department he'd fast-track on his public service career with a jump to vice mayor. Having retreated to Canyon Springs after the Macy misfortune, he figured he was now five years behind on his plan to reach the state capitol by the time he was forty. Nevertheless, he'd worked hard to establish himself and gain the townspeople's respect before running for city council.

He pulled the white cross from his pocket and held it in the palm of his hand, tilting it so it glistened in the lamplight. How many times had he seen Granddad pull it from his own pocket and rub it thoughtfully between his forefinger and thumb? Made from Hawaiian seashell, he'd once told him. When Granddad died, Grandma asked what he'd like to have that belonged to him. Without hesitation, he'd said the cross.

He momentarily fisted the symbolic object in his hand, then slid it back into his pocket. Slipping into his suit jacket and straightening his tie, he then headed to the door. He'd walk to the fund-raiser tonight. Maybe it would clear the cobwebs out of his head.

Usually he took Grandma to these things, but with her still out of town he'd declined to substitute with a date. A few weeks ago he might have asked Paris, but she'd have her hands full behind the scenes at the big community event. Besides, they probably didn't have as much in common as he'd once imagined.

Twenty minutes later, Larry James waved him over, making urgent motions from where he stood near a table in the softly lit high school gymnasium. Now what? From the look of suppressed excitement on his face, Jake wasn't sure he wanted to know.

As his eyes adjusted to the light, he maneuvered around high school-aged servers dressed in black, then glanced to the head table, where Macy sat next to the president of the chamber of commerce. Several other men, including Paris's father, crowded around to chat with her. He grimaced. Since when were they fans of a blog filled with recipes, snippets of local history and lively homespun anecdotes?

Macy's hair, loosely upswept, shone softly and her jeweled earrings sparkled, enhancing her shimmering black halter dress. Did she take fancy outfits along with her wherever she went? She all but glowed as she chatted animatedly with those around her. Still staring at her as he made his way through the crowd, Jake almost bumped into Larry.

"Uh, sorry. What's up?"

His friend leaned in, voice low. "The mayor and his Mrs. had a little mishap."

"What kind of mishap?"

"Car trouble on the way up the mountain from Phoenix." He looked more elated than news of that sort should elicit. "They may get here late. Maybe not. He needs someone to fill in for him tonight."

"Master of ceremonies? Give a speech you mean?"

"Don and I think you're the man for the job." Larry nudged him. "Faster on your verbal feet than either of us and never short on appropriate words for any occasion. And you know how Bernie and Hector hate getting up in front of a crowd. Gus says it doesn't have to be fancy. A basic welcome and introducing the performers and guest speaker. Can you manage that?"

He could, but he hadn't planned to do more than put in an appearance this evening, then slip away. It had been an exhausting week and tonight was more than irritating with men clustering around Macy. But how could he say no?

"Yeah, sure. I can do it."

Larry thrust an elegantly scripted five-by-seven card into his hands. "Here. This should keep you on track."

Jake glanced at the program, then at his watch. "Looks like we have about twenty minutes until show time."

He turned to where he knew his assigned seat was; council and chamber members were presiding at various tables. But his friend nabbed his arm.

"Uh, Jake?"

"Yeah?"

Larry jerked his head toward the front of the auditorium. "You'll need to sit at the head table. Up near the stage. We can't have you crawling over the top of folks every time it's your turn to speak."

The head table. With Macy.

"You can sit at Gus's place. Shouldn't be too much of a hardship to be right next to the guest of honor, should it?" Larry chuckled. "You know, seeing as how you couldn't get yourself a date."

Jake ignored the familiar jab. "Would you get word to my table that I've been recruited for other duties? Maybe pull someone in to cover for me?"

"Will do. Now you'd better get yourself on over there before that poor little blog lady's bored out of her mind by chamber talk."

Jake straightened his shirt cuffs, then made his way toward the dais in front of the stage, stopping among the elegantly-decorated tables to shake hands and share a word with the guests who'd generously contributed toward the event.

It appeared, even at twenty-five dollars a ticket, to be a record turnout for the dessert night. Paris had outdone herself. You'd never guess this classy venue with its flickering faux candlelight reflecting off borrowed china and crystal was a high school gym. Amazingly, she'd managed to filter out the eau-de-athletic socks scent with an abundance of fresh flowers, thanks to Bernie's generosity, no doubt. But he couldn't fool himself; the big draw was Macy.

Arriving at the head table elevated on a low dais, he wormed his way to the empty chair next to Macy. Her groupies scattered and his heart swelled when she looked up at him, a flicker of pleased surprise in her eyes.

"Good evening everyone." He nodded to the four couples seated at the table. How much extra had they paid for the best seats in the house? "We have a slight change in plans. It seems our illustrious mayor and his better half have been delayed. I'll be covering for him and, if there are no major objections, I'll join you for dinner, as well."

He didn't look at Macy and the bare-shouldered black dress. Maybe it hadn't been such a good idea to seat her here at the head table where everyone in the room could gawk at her. Maybe he could get her moved to an inconspicuous corner in the high school's kitchen.

"Aw, sit yourself down, Jake. You know you're always welcome." Chamber of commerce president Al Keene nodded his thinning-haired head toward Macy. "I bet this pretty lady will enjoy your company a sight more than she has mine."

The ladies around him giggled. All except Macy, who only smiled as graciously as he'd have expected. She was similar to Paris in that respect, cool and unruffled when she found it to her advantage to be.

"That remains to be seen, Al." He pulled out the chair next to her and seated himself, offering her what he hoped was a reassuring smile. "But I'll do my best."

"Then I'd better give Macy fair warning before Jake turns on the charm." Al's wife Hilary leaned in with a conspiratorial whisper. "You know, in case no one's clued her in that this is Canyon Springs's most eligible bachelor."

Amusement lit Macy's eyes as she turned to him. "Then I'll have to be on my guard, won't I?"

Al slapped the tabletop, startling Macy. "I imagine being on guard isn't what most females hereabouts think of when hoping Jake will come calling."

Jake glanced uncertainly at Macy. You had to have a thick skin to deal with those who thought they had the right to make judgments and share observations on your personal life.

Hilary elbowed her husband. "Stop that. You're making her blush."

"She looks mighty pretty doing it, too." Al propped an elbow on the table and, squinting one eye, shook his finger at Jake. "With Gus out of the way this evening, you've got her all to yourself, mister. Better make the most of it."

Chapter Thirteen

All to himself? That was a stretch with the eyes of those seated around the table—and maybe throughout the gym—riveted expectantly on the two of them.

Macy hadn't missed the wink one of the men gave Jake to confirm Al's directive. Poor Jake. In her public role as a popular blogger she'd endured the meddling of matchmakers and heard more than her fair share of well-intentioned jokes at her expense. She seldom stayed more than two weeks, maybe a month, in one place, but Jake had lived here many years. The teasing had to get old.

A stylishly coiffed woman—Alisa?—seated next to the chamber president's wife gave her a sympathetic look and changed the subject. "Jake, how is your grandmother? Is she planning to come back to Canyon Springs or stay in Phoenix with your sister's family? We were wondering if it's too hard for her here without your grandfather."

"She's a tough old gal." Jake sounded proud of

her. "I imagine she'll be back before it gets too hot in the Valley."

"I'm glad to hear it. The next time you talk to her, please tell her we miss her."

Others murmured agreement.

"I'll do that. I know she misses everyone here, too."

The woman then again deftly redirected the table conversation to the high school track team's recent achievements. Thank goodness for sports.

Macy used the opportunity to turn to Jake, who seemed intent on studying something or someone across the room. Paris? He'd said he wasn't seeing her, but relationships had been known to mysteriously change overnight and she hadn't spoken to him for days. She touched his arm lightly to get his attention, keeping her voice low.

"How was your day?" She couldn't help but notice how his clean-cut good looks were enhanced by the charcoal suit, white shirt and burgundy tie. No doubt she wasn't the only woman there tonight who'd taken notice as he'd passed by.

"Good. Good. And yours?"

"Busy. There's a load of stock to unpack at the Warehouse with *seasonal guests* soon to arrive." He returned her smile, noticing that she'd remembered the politically correct terminology he'd shared earlier. Her spirits rose. "Customers are stopping in more frequently, too. Sharon says they're early birds who want to catch a prime campground or cabin spot."

"Or they've been reading your blog and didn't want to miss meeting you. You had quite a following gathered here before I broke things up."

He leaned in slightly, his jacketed arm brushing hers, and she caught the familiar scent of his aftershave. He'd seldom been this close to her in the past other than when he'd kissed her. How effortless it would be to now lift her face to his and...

"It looked to be getting a little crowded," he added.

If she didn't know better, she'd think Jake was jealous.

"It wasn't how it appeared. Those men were trying to talk me into featuring local real estate businesses this week and providing links to their websites."

"Excuses, excuses." His now-husky voice lowered further. "Just a reason to chat with a beautiful woman."

That was the second time he'd slipped that compliment into a conversation recently. Hadn't they come to an understanding that God had closed the door? That nothing had changed between them in the intervening years? So why was he wasting effort on flattering remarks? Nevertheless, they buoyed her spirits.

"But I guess," he continued, "that real estate explains Paris's dad Merle hovering around."

"Merle?" She remembered the distinguished gentleman. "I hadn't caught his last name."

"Well-to-do widower." Jake gave her a sidelong glance, impish lights dancing in his eyes. "You could do worse, Macy."

"Oh, you." She fisted her fingers and gave his arm a gentle punch. "Don't you go matchmaking, too."

As if suddenly aware of where they were, Jake straightened, suppressed a grin and glanced at his watch—something she noticed he did frequently these days. Then he stood.

"I know your introduction is scheduled for later, but we may as well introduce you now. Ninety-nine percent of the people here came to get a look at the creator of *Hometowns With Heart,* not to eat a piece of homemade pie they can get at any church potluck. Let's not make them wait."

He held out his hand to her and she self-consciously slipped hers into his strong warm one for the first time in years. He gave it a gentle squeeze and their gazes met as the familiar touch sparked memories she'd long censored. Quiet evenings studying at the library. Hot chocolate shared at a coffeehouse table. Kisses stolen in the shadows outside her dormitory's entrance.

She rose to her feet and he, almost reluctantly, released her hand and motioned her toward the stage steps.

The rest of the evening whirled into a blur of delicious desserts and a choral music presentation of tunes from the sixties and seventies. Her talk about her blogging life and words of encouragement to hang on to what made Canyon Springs special seemed well received. Small talk filled the hours as well, both at her table and later as she made her way around the room with Jake at her side to meet those who'd come out to support a good cause. Occasionally he'd lean in, his hand brushing the small of her back, to whisper a few words, his breath soft against her ear.

In those moments it took effort to remain focused on her guest of honor duties.

By ten o'clock, the two of them had given their thank-yous at the podium. After the crowd thinned, she personally sought out Paris and Sharon to thank them for their combined efforts in making the evening a success. As the volunteers started cleanup, Jake pulled her aside.

"You're not expected to stay and help." His gaze sought hers in what could only be described as cautious anticipation and her heart beat faster. "I'd be happy to walk you to your lodging if you'd like."

Jake held his breath. She didn't answer immediately, obviously debating the wisdom of a nighttime trek with him. "It's not too far and the wind died down this afternoon. It might give you a chance to unwind and see Canyon Springs at a slower pace."

"Canyon Springs has a slower pace?" A soft smile touched her lips, then she nodded. "A walk would be nice."

An invisible band suddenly tightened around his chest, a school-boyish tension at the thought of walking a pretty girl home at night. Why'd she say yes? Why had she paused before answering? What would they talk about that wouldn't once again end up putting them at odds?

Lord, is this an opportunity You're providing or am I interfering? He could have asked one of the other council members to see her home. How were you supposed to know when you should "step out on faith" and take the initiative or step back and let things take their own course?

She retrieved her shawl and handbag, then he escorted her out a side door. No point in drawing attention to their departure. He touched her arm lightly, guiding her down the dimly-lit steps toward the sidewalk.

The cool night air smelled faintly of ponderosas and the underlying tang of pinyon pine woodsmoke. Stars sparkled in a cloudless sky as they left behind the high school's illumination and moved farther into the residential area. Lights glowed softly from the windows of homes, lending the street a cozy feeling.

"Chilly tonight. Is that shawl enough for you? It's hardly bigger than a scrap."

"I'm fine."

But he was already peeling out of his suit jacket, slipping it around her slim shoulders before she could protest.

"Thank you."

"You're welcome."

They walked along in silence, passing by porch-fronted homes and under the branches of trees not quite leafed out. It was a far cry from the warm evening when they'd last strolled the University of Missouri campus, their fingers intertwined. For a fleeting second he almost reached for her hand. But no. Just because he was feeling nostalgic, there'd be no guarantee she would be, too, or that his touch would be welcomed. While the tension between them had ebbed and flowed since her arrival in Canyon Springs, they were still miles apart in many realms.

"You seem to have quite the reputation as a ladies' man, Mr. Talford."

He caught the teasing lilt in her voice, the curiosity in her words. "Totally unearned, I assure you. Al likes listening to himself talk and doesn't know when to put a lid on it. I hope he didn't embarrass you. He gets carried away."

"I actually thought he was kind of funny. Harmless." She looked up at him. "But I was afraid he might be making *you* uncomfortable."

"Mostly out of concern for you. As we've touched on earlier, it's awkward with no one knowing we knew each other previously, which maybe makes people's comments seem more pointed to us than they are."

"True." He could hear the smile in her voice. "Like Al's parting shot about your mandate to steal a goodnight kiss?"

"Having no idea we've been there, done that."

"And have no intention," she said firmly, "of doing it again."

"Right." He shoved his hands into his trouser pockets as they continued on to the rhythm of their foot-steps on the pavement. So she had no intention of kissing him ever again. Sensible decision. Now if only he could stop thinking about the last time they *did* kiss. Before things fell apart. It had nagged at him all evening.

Like tonight, they'd walked around campus, one of their favorite pastimes when a day's classes and an evening of studying at the library had come to a close. MU was a big campus, a blend of modern-styled buildings and those from the 1800s orna-mented by arching trees, grassy lawns and winding walkways. He'd never forget the scent of the campus lush with May greenery.

Hand in hand, they'd crossed The Quad in front of the Ionic columns, all that remained of the fire-damaged, pre-Civil War Academic Hall. The dome of Jesse Hall had risen in stately majesty behind them.

And the whole while, he couldn't take his mind off the engagement ring he'd left secured under his mattress. His plan had been to drive Macy to a bluff overlooking the mighty Missouri River the evening before graduation, only a few days away.

What if he would've had the ring with him that night? Had spoken the words he'd rehearsed? Would it have made a difference? Not likely. The end was already written in God's book—and in newspaper print. The article had come out the next day.

"Was that a sigh, Jake?" she asked softly.

"What? No. Just breathing in the mountain air." He'd better keep his focus on the here and now.

"It's invigorating isn't it? Much different from the mellow, earthy scent of mid-Missouri vegetation this time of year."

Had she been thinking about that night, too? About them? "Both are beautiful parts of the country in their own way."

"I know you didn't live there long, but do you ever…miss Missouri?"

One part of it. Her part.

He jangled the few coins in his pocket, his fingertips brushing Granddad's cross. "I have to admit it was nice to throw a few seeds on the ground and have them grow up almost overnight. It's risky to plant anything here before Memorial Day for fear of a freeze, and lawns in this dry mountain soil are too much work."

She didn't respond and he sensed that wasn't what her question was meant to draw from him. She hadn't been looking for an agricultural comparison.

Idiot. As in the past, he'd automatically evaded her, unwilling to open himself to a more vulnerable exchange even though he himself had been yearning for that very thing only moments ago.

Garnering his courage, he adjusted his jacket more securely around her shoulders. "Funny you should mention Missouri since I was just thinking about the walks we used to take around campus."

There, he'd gotten it out in the open.

"The flora and the fauna?"

Now she was doing it. Taking her cue from his inane comments. Distancing herself.

"Actually…" *Come on, Talford, crawl out of that crusty hard shell of yours.* He took a rallying breath. Then, to his disgust, he realized they'd come to the bed and breakfast where Macy now resided.

Stomach in knots, he motioned her up the curving path, thankful the porch boasted no glaring overhead lights. Instead, low solar-powered orbs provided visibility along the brick walkway, dainty stained glass butterflies atop them. On impulse, he reached for her hand.

"Macy."

She turned slowly, her questioning eyes seeking his. His heart beat faster.

"I think everyone enjoyed meeting you tonight. Your talk was encouraging and I think you made everyone proud to be one of your *Hometowns With Heart.*"

"Thank you. I meant every word. Canyon Springs is special."

A smile tugged. "Aw, I bet you say that to all your hometowns."

Her melodic laugh caressed his ears. "I do, but I can honestly say Canyon Springs is extra special."

"I'm glad you think so." He gave her hand a gentle squeeze. "I had a nice evening as well, spending it with you."

She nodded. Was that a "me, too" or only an acknowledgment of his statement?

"Maybe we could do it again sometime. Soon." There, he'd done it. Opened the door to something more personal. Would she slam it in his face? Was God frowning from on high that he refused to take no for an answer?

Her lips twitched slightly. "You have charity dinners often around here, do you?"

"We probably would if we had you for a keynote speaker."

"I'd probably sound like a broken record if I had to do it on a regular basis. Limited repertoire."

"That's doubtful." He held her gaze for a long moment. "Macy—"

She broke eye contact, then glanced back at him, her expression a mix of longing and fear. Exactly what he was experiencing at the moment.

He stepped closer, cradling her hand in his. So soft. Warm. He gave it a reassuring squeeze, his gaze lowering to her lips, then back to her hope-filled, luminous eyes. She wanted this as much as he did. He sensed it.

Her breath coming rapidly, she shyly let her gaze drift to the soft lighting along the walkway and he drew courage to step even closer. Lean in...

"Oh." Abruptly she stepped back and pulled her hand from his, then almost frantically shrugged out of his jacket. "I guess you'd like to have this back, wouldn't you?"

She thrust it into his hands.

Dazed, he stared at her, gut-socked.

"Good night, Jake." She hurried up the steps to the B and B.

Chapter Fourteen

Jake had tried to kiss her.

And if it hadn't been for those stupid stained glass butterflies on the walkway lights, she'd have let him. *Stop chasing butterflies. Stop chasing butterflies.* The voice in her head wouldn't shut up and instead of kissing him she'd flung his jacket at him and left him standing there in a stupor.

Now in her second-story room overlooking the tree-lined street, she didn't turn on the lights but hurried to the window. Peeking between the lacy curtains she could see no sign of him. What did she think he'd do? Stand gazing up at her window like a lovesick pup? Throw a brick through it?

Her cell phone sounded in the silence, sending her heart scampering.

Jake?

She scrambled for her purse in the dark, dumping its contents on the bedspread and fumbling to locate the telltale blinking green light. Spotting it, she snatched up her phone. No, not Jake. Her sister. She inhaled deeply, exhaled slowly. For a moment she considered not answering, but she'd tried that before. Nicole wouldn't leave a message, she'd just keep calling.

"You sound breathless," Nicole pointed out the obvious when Macy picked up.

"I just got back from a fund-raiser. Ran up the stairs. It takes some adjusting to this high elevation." She lowered herself onto the four-poster bed, still trembling from her encounter with Jake. "What are you doing up so late?"

"Late? It's only two o'clock on a Saturday morning here in the Big Apple. The night is young."

"So what's up?" Macy squeezed her eyes shut, praying for a short and painless conversation.

"Vanessa called earlier this evening. She's keeping an eye on your blog and wondered again when we're going to see some action."

Action. As in something more edgy. More newsworthy.

"This is a small town. Front page news can be pretty mundane. But my research is laying the groundwork."

Or at least she hoped it would. Thus far perusing the local paper revealed only that the food bank needed donations to replenish its stock and the care facility had changed ownership. Even the police report hadn't coughed up anything more significant than a no proof of insurance citation and an expired driver's license.

"A few weeks ago you said you thought there was a juicy story hidden in the closet of every little town. Vanessa & Company are getting antsy. Mom is, too."

"You want me to fabricate something?"

"Of course not. But Mom's afraid you're cozying into the hometown turf too much. You know, the bakery stuff, the weddings. She doesn't think you're making the best use of your time."

Irritation flared as Macy rose from the bed to pace the floor. Mom, who hadn't written a single news story in over thirty-five years, now had all the answers. But immediately she tamped down the hot words threatening to spill forth. Mom was her mentor. She was looking out for her daughter's best interests.

"Remember, sis, events like the fund-raiser not only create goodwill on behalf of my blog, they let me get to know townspeople and them to know me. That makes them more apt to share community matters that might not be revealed to an outsider."

Like that argument she'd heard between Reuben Falkner and Jake? A former councilman challenging a current one could possibly prove controversial enough if it was played up sufficiently. But no way would she pursue that. Jake would see it as overstepping the boundaries, as betrayal.

"Well don't *you* forget, Macy, this hometown visit has more riding on it than any of them in the past."

Macy's lips tightened. "Believe me, forgetting would be a little hard to do considering I hear from you or Mom every other day. Tell everyone to sit back and relax, okay? Trust me."

Undoubtedly Nicole had more to say on the subject, but after a prolonged silence she said good-night and hung up.

Macy tossed her phone on the bed, then returned to the window, raising it before lowering herself onto the cushioned seat. Cool air crept in and she reached for a crocheted afghan, slipping its soft folds around her shoulders. It warmed her just as Jake's jacket had a short while ago.

"Lord, what am I going to do?" she whispered as she stared out at the quiet night. How could it be so serene when inside she was in such turmoil? "Everyone is counting on me to do something big and splashy. Something my sponsor can use to justify investing in the potential of my blog."

She pulled the crocheted comforter closer. "If You don't give me any ideas, any tips to follow up on, I'm going to fall flat on my face. My mother will be mad at me. My sister won't get a cut on the contracts to reward her for what she's done on my behalf. My main sponsor will probably dump me altogether. I'll let everyone down."

Not too far away, a dog barked and she leaned forward. Was it Jake, walking Abe after having returned home? She rested her forehead against the cool, glass pane in an attempt to see as far down the street as she could.

No sign of anyone. Disappointed, she leaned back, propping herself up with a throw pillow.

"And what about Jake?" she murmured. "I so badly wanted to kiss him." Would that have been chasing butterflies again? By sending Jake packing, had she just passed a test with flying colors or miserably failed one?

No heavenly whispers responded in the stillness. Nevertheless, deep down inside she knew the answer. Jake was practically married to this little town and her future lay far from here, especially if she delivered what her sponsor demanded. Besides, what would Jake's reaction be when this elusive idea for a going-out-with-a-bang blog post materialized? It would undoubtedly involve someone in his precious community, past or present, and he wouldn't approve.

"I'm in a no-win situation, Lord."

She closed her eyes, breath quickening, momentarily reliving those fleeting moments when Jake had looked deep into her eyes and taken her hand. Moved in slowly, cautiously...

With a last, lingering look out the window, she pushed aside the afghan and stood, then pulled down the shade.

"Come on, Abe, get a move on." Flashlight in hand, Jake tugged on the beagle's leash, determined to burn off excess energy after that humiliating con-

clusion to a promising evening. He'd stopped at home
to change clothes, then deliberately set off in the op-
posite direction from the B and B where Macy was
staying.

Boy had he blown it.

How had he misread the signals? Had they been
wishful thinking? Hallucination?

What must Macy think of him?

No wonder she'd panicked. He'd acted as if no
time had passed between them and he was entitled
to step up and give her a kiss just because he wanted
to. He'd made it no secret when she came to town
that he didn't trust her, so talk about your mixed
messages. Wasn't he still checking her blog for anything that crossed the line? Expecting her to pull a
fast one as she'd done six years ago? He was lucky
she'd only flung off his jacket rather than socking
him in the jaw.

He gave Abe's leash another tug. "Get your nose
out of that log, Abe, and let's get on home."

The dog looked up at him, wagged his tail and together they headed down the starlit street. He'd made
a bad choice tonight. There was no way around it. As
sweet as it would have been to end the evening with
Macy in his arms, it would have implied something
he wasn't ready to commit to.

He'd have to call to let her know the financial outcome of the fund-raiser when that had been determined, but from then on out he'd renew his original
vow to keep as far away from her as he could.

* * *

"Thanks, Ava, that sounds interesting." Monday morning Macy stared across the almost-empty discount store parking lot where she'd pulled in only moments before to answer her phone. "I know you've been busy, but have you found anything more on our Canyon Springs Dexter that would shed light on the mystery twosome?"

"Not much. Are you where you can pull up the email I just sent? I attached the clipping that announced my Dexter and his buddy entering the navy. I thought you might want to see what he looked like."

Macy quickly logged on to her email through her phone and opened the attachment. It was a remarkably clear black-and-white photo of two young men in their late teens smiling proudly for the camera. Dexter Smith and Tommy O'Donner, the caption read.

A cold finger curled up her spine as she stared at Tommy's familiar face. "Ava…the caption is messed up. This guy labeled Tommy O'Donner is my Dexter Smith."

"No way, sweetie. Your Dexter died last year. This one died in 1941."

"I know you said that, but something's goofed up." She tilted the phone's screen to shade it from the sunlight's glare. "Remember the article at the museum where I got his name? It had a photo of him. He's obviously younger here and doesn't…" In the museum photo he'd appeared to have a scarred-over eye injury. "I'm certain this is my Dexter Smith. The build. The shape of his face. The hair. The smile."

"I don't see how that can be."

Macy continued to stare at the photo. "I'll take a digital of the museum clipping and send it to you and see what you think. There must be a mistake in this article. The identifying caption got switched or something. Maybe the information you found on your Dexter's death was wrong. Maybe it was his friend— this Tommy guy—who died, not him."

"I can recheck…" Ava sounded reluctant and Macy instantly regretted challenging her findings.

"Maybe there's a retraction about the earlier report of his death," she suggested tactfully. "I'm sure the news coming in after the attack on Pearl Harbor wouldn't always have been accurate."

"Unfortunately, retractions don't make the front page news."

"I'm sorry, Ava, but I'm sure this is my Dexter." Pleased that she might have a lead on him even though it wasn't blog worthy, the two friends said their goodbyes. Macy headed into the discount store, wishing there was more to the Dexter Smith story than a case of misreporting. Maybe then it would have taken her mind off Jake.

After a few sleepless nights, she could only come to one conclusion about Friday evening's romantic interlude. While he'd been more than frank about his inability to trust her, Jake had clearly expected her to be receptive to his advances, just as she'd been years ago when she'd been young and naive enough to go along with a relationship that had no ties, no commitments, no future. His behavior was the equivalent of an old TV rerun where nothing changed no matter how many times you watched it. She was right to have refused his attempted caress.

It had been a test and she'd passed.

Refocusing on the mission at hand, Macy reached for a bottle of shampoo on the shelf. She'd knocked hers over that morning, not noticing until she'd lost three-quarters of it down the drain. She placed the generic brand back on the shelf and selected another one, attempting to concentrate on the fine print.

But what if…there *could* be a future for her and Jake? What if he came to trust her? Finally managed to broach a long-term commitment? Would she be willing to give him a chance? To her disgust, she kept coming back to that question.

Lord, how did I get into this mess?

She couldn't deny she still had feelings for him, and she suspected he had feelings for her, as well. The time spent with him Friday night had been wonderful. His whispered words. The longing looks. His light touch at the small of her back. It had been almost as if a golden bubble surrounded them, invisibly shutting out the rest of the world. There had been a sense that although they shared a table with other couples, they were there alone. Just the two of them…

"I tell you, Bill, that Jake Talford is something else. Going above and beyond in my book."

Macy squeezed the shampoo bottle tightly in her hand when the familiar voice one aisle over mentioned Jake's name.

"That's why we voted him in, isn't it, Mr. Mayor?"

"That we did." Gus Gustoffsen chuckled, and she could almost envision the tall man pulling out his handkerchief and wiping his brow. "I hear he came through for us at the fund-raiser. I can't give him all the credit for it, though. It was really all my doing."

Macy glanced down the aisle to make sure she was the only one in it, then moved closer to the shelving to listen. Anything having to do with Jake justified eavesdropping.

"And what is it you're taking credit for?" the man who'd been called Bill responded.

Gus chuckled again. "I put a bug in his ear a few weeks ago, suggesting it might benefit our community—and his future in local politics—if he'd do a little pitchin' woo to Miss Macy Colston."

The air squeezed from Macy's lungs. She almost dropped the bottle.

"You know," the mayor continued jovially, "to make sure she puts a positive spin on us. What's better than a romantic haze to color her perceptions?"

"He went along with it?" The other man's voice echoed doubt. "Doesn't sound like Jake to me."

"Well…he refused at first, but from what I've picked up this past week or so, he's seeing the wisdom of it. He has a vested interest in that vice mayor opening, you know. As I hear it, Jake grabbed my conveniently timed car trouble and ran with it. From all reports, he outdid himself. In fact, he had her eating out of his hand."

With trembling fingers, Macy replaced the shampoo bottle on the shelf, unwilling to hear any more. She had to get out of here. Now.

Briskly moving down the aisle, barely able to draw a breath, she rushed for the main exit as a roaring in her ears muffled all other sounds.

Did everyone at the fund-raiser know this? That Jake and the mayor colluded to win her favor on behalf of the town? Is that what the teasing remarks had been about? Had they been watching, nodding knowingly, when he'd joined them at the table? Did they snicker to themselves when he'd leaned in close to whisper a few words? Maybe they'd lurked in the bushes outside the high school and given each other high fives when he whisked her off for a walk to her lodging, knowing his plan was to end the evening with a kiss.

She swallowed back the growing lump in her throat as reality crowded in, a blindfold being removed from her eyes. Jake wasn't as innocent in setting up the tour of the town as he'd originally appeared to be. He'd known all along Gus would bow out as guide and he'd step in. The encounter at Hector's—had he set that up, too?

And the flowers…?

Had he broken up with Paris or was that part of the ruse?

As she passed rapidly by the checkout counters, hot waves of humiliation rolled over her. The sliding glass exit door couldn't open fast enough.

And then, at last, she was outside, gulping in the fresh, cool air.

What did I do to deserve this, God?

She'd no more than reached her car and jerked open the door when her cell phone rang. She fumbled with her purse to silence it, then checked caller ID.

Jake.

Tears welled as she rammed the phone back into her purse, but she blinked them away. She intended to talk to Jake all right. But only after she had time to think. To pray. She wouldn't make a phone call, though. He'd have to hear face-to-face every single word she had to say.

Chapter Fifteen

"Why don't you give it up, Jake?" asked Joe Diaz, a pal from church and the men's Bible study. Joe had crossed his path half a mile back and had joined him on a late afternoon run. "Why not let them do whatever they want to do with the property? As they say, you can't fight city hall."

Jake glanced down at Abe, galloping along the forest trail beside them, floppy ears flying. The little guy loved these outings. "I don't think that's what Granddad would have wanted."

"For them to sell it? Or for you to give up?"

"Neither."

Joe picked up the pace and Jake followed suit, his lungs pumping in the thin mountain air.

"What's your grandma say?"

"She said he gave it to the city. Period."

"Then it sounds as if she'd be good with the town selling it and you should be, too."

Jake grimaced. "But it's her and Granddad's first home."

"And he bought her a bigger and better one later, didn't he?" Obviously Joe thought this was a no-brainer. "Sounds as if you're more sentimental about it than she is."

"Maybe. But Granddad could have torn it down and built a new place right on the same acreage." Jake's muscles pumped as he lengthened his stride, his breath coming evenly. "He didn't, which tells me it meant something to him, too. I think I let him down when I didn't buy it from him when I moved here."

"He didn't leave it to you though, did he?" Joe ran a hand through his sweat-dampened hair and glanced Jake's way. "He didn't put any stipulations on it for city use, so why should you?"

"Because I don't want to see someone putting in a liquor store, tattoo parlor or a tobacco shop— three things that would make Granddad roll over in his grave." He easily leaped over a downed limb in their path. Joe skirted around it. "Whoever bought it would probably tear down the house and rebuild on the land."

"Then that could be a problem."

They ran along in silence, Abe loping at Jake's side.

"Changing the subject…" Joe said at last, his tone hesitant. "What's this I hear about you courting Macy Colston on orders from the mayor?"

Jake stumbled, then righted himself and made up the lost ground. "What are you talking about?"

"My dad said the mayor caught him at the discount store this morning, bragging about how you'll hands down be picked to replace Parker as vice mayor and win reelection in a few years if you can pull this off."

Jake's stomach lurched. Apparently Gus thought Jake had come over to his point of view. "Come on. You know Gus."

Joe's stride slowed and Jake reluctantly matched his pace. "So you're not seeing her on behalf of the town? Trying to get her to treat us right on that blog of hers?"

"No."

"I'm glad to hear you say that. She seems like a nice lady. I'd hate to see her get hurt."

"Nobody has plans to hurt her, Joe." He drew to a halt. Joe did likewise.

Bending over to catch his breath, his hands braced above his knees, Jake looked over at his friend. "I'd rather this didn't get around, but so you know, Macy and I…"

How to explain it? The situation had been complicated. He didn't care to share details. He certainly didn't want Joe looking down on him for having once lowered his guard and compromised his integrity.

"Macy and you what?"

Jake straightened. "We knew each other when I was at the University of Missouri, not long before I moved to Canyon Springs. But we hadn't seen each other since then. Not until now."

"As in you were *seeing* each other?" Joe gave him an evaluating look. "Dating?"

Jake shrugged. "Yeah. Dating."

"What happened?"

"Things didn't work out. We broke up. So I can tell you right now, any rumors you hear that I've set out to romance her for the good of the town are false. That would be flat-out foolish with the history we have between us."

A corner of Joe's mouth lifted. "And you've never been a foolish man, have you?"

Only once. With Macy.

"Not when I can help it."

He'd almost imprudently tumbled down the same hole a few nights ago, but he wouldn't be going there again. Macy didn't want any part of it and now that he had time to knock some sense into his own head, he wouldn't be venturing out again in that direction.

With the shadows growing longer, Jake set off walking for a cooldown, hoping to divert Joe from further questioning. He glanced at his friend. "Now it's my turn to change the subject. How's Meg feeling? Won't be long and she'll be a mom for the first time."

The proud papa grinned. "She's feeling great now, but is getting big as a barrel. Well, you saw her at church."

"You're ready to be a dad again?"

Joe cut him a curious look. "Before Meg, I didn't think I'd ever be. I wasn't around much when Davy was small. The navy was my life. But now?" His grin broadened. "I'm more than ready."

Jake rolled his shoulders as he gazed up at the tree-tops. "I've always wondered if I'm not married because I'd make a lousy husband and father and God knows it. My folks didn't exactly set the best example of a stable home life."

"Mine neither, remember?"

That's right. Joe had once told him his mother had abandoned him and his father when Joe was fifteen years old. She'd taken his two younger siblings with her.

Joe clapped Jake on the shoulder. "Hey man, don't let the mistakes your parents made hold you back when you find the right woman. Trust God, learn from what your parents did wrong and do better. Turn things around for the next generation."

When they parted ways, Jake headed for home with Abe, his memory again lingering on his walk with Macy Friday night. It had felt so right—up until the end, that is. Joe sounded certain the husband and father thing could be done with God's help. That's assuming, though, that both people were going in the same direction.

Had he let his parents' mistakes hold him back? Is that why he'd been slow to move ahead in the relationship? Could his experiences have caused him to miss out on a special woman because he'd learned the hard way to avoid commitments that didn't come with guarantees? Or had the breakup been divine intervention?

"Come on, Abe." Glimpsing his A-frame through a thick stand of ponderosas, he broke into a jog for the final stretch home. He'd barely hit the clearing when he noticed a car in the driveway—and Macy standing on the front deck.

His spirits rose at the sight of her golden hair cascading over her shoulders, the fading pinkish hues of sunset illuminating her features. His heart hammered in expectation. She looked like a dream.

Or she would have if it weren't for the folded arms and the angry glint in her eyes directed at him.

"Councilman Talford—" she said as she lifted her chin "—I want to have a word with you."

Abe—now grown up and as adorable as ever— bounded toward her, tail wagging furiously. But his master followed at a slower pace, eyeing her with caution.

As well he should.

"What's up, Macy?" Dressed for a run, he placed a tennis-shoed foot on the bottom step, but didn't venture to join her on the deck. "Would you care to come in? I think there's lemonade in—"

"No, I would not, thank you." Abe bumped against her leg, vying for attention, but she didn't take her eyes off Jake. "What I have to say will only take a minute."

She was determined to get through this without

shedding any tears. There had been enough of those in the privacy of her car as she drove the rental around for hours that afternoon.

"Ohhkay." He gestured to the Adirondack chairs on the deck. "Would you like to sit down then?"

"No, I would not." If he thought he could sidetrack her, employ that charm of his, he had another think coming.

"What seems to be the problem?"

"As if you didn't know." How could he stand there and act innocent? "Why don't you tell me about this plot you and the mayor hatched? The plan you orchestrated to win me over to Canyon Springs with, shall we say, personal attention?"

His eyes widened slightly. "I didn't hatch any plans to do that."

"No? Well, reconsider that denial. This morning I heard the mayor bragging on how he'd gotten you to 'romance' me so I'd be persuaded to put a positive spin on the community and give you a boost in local politics. Vice mayor, is it?"

He stepped onto the deck. "I didn't—"

She backed up, almost tripping over Abe. "I don't appreciate being made fool of. To know the whole town is in on it, watching and cheering from the sidelines as you made your moves on their behalf."

He stretched out his hand in appeal. "I did not—"

"Come on, Jake, why not admit it? The mayor is proud of you for, as he put it, getting me to eat out of your hand. He said you outdid yourself the other night when he 'conveniently' had car trouble. What did you do? Report to him the moment you left me? I'm sure it was a disappointment for him, for the entire town, that you didn't score a kiss."

"Now, Macy—" He took a step toward her, but she raised a hand to hold him off.

"Let me finish, Jake. Do you have any idea how humiliating it is to know all eyes were on me at the fund-raiser, not because I was the guest of honor but because the two of us were everyone's *entertainment* for the evening? Eyes were glued to see if I'd fall for your smooth-talking shenanigans. Everyone watching to see if you'd get me to take a walk home that would end in a kiss. Thank goodness I didn't let you get away with that."

"You've got this all wrong."

Wrong? She hadn't made up what the mayor said and she hadn't mistaken Jake's intentions when they'd reached the B and B.

She placed fisted hands on her hips. "You intended to kiss me and don't you dare deny it."

"I don't deny it. But the rest of this is twisted around."

"Didn't you hear what I said? I heard the mayor myself!" Her voice cracked a little and she swallowed hard, forcing back the tears that wanted to rise again. "I know you've always had political aspirations, so I suppose it's not all that surprising he talked you into this pseudo romance stunt to pave the way to your future."

"Macy, please." He drew closer, his blue eyes darkening as he reached for her hand, but she pulled away and backed up a few more steps.

"You know what's most sad?" A halfhearted laugh escaped her throat. "I like Canyon Springs. Or I did until this humiliating episode. I thought immediately this was a special place with special people. But apparently there's more going on below the surface than what meets the eye."

He took another step toward her and she backed up again, bumping against the French door. With a chair to her left and a table to her right and Jake smack in front of her, she suddenly realized that she'd allowed herself to be trapped.

"Now it's your turn to listen to me, Macy." His voice had taken on a deadly tone that sent prickles racing up her spine. "You said this would only take a minute of my time. What I have to say will only take a minute of yours."

She clenched her jaw, eyes narrowing, determined not to let him intimidate her. "There's nothing you can say or do to redeem yourself. You played me for a fool in front of the whole town."

And even worse, he'd made her think about what it might be like to have him back in her life again.

He drew a slow breath, obviously calling on his most lawyerlike depths of patience as his solemn gaze captured and held hers. "I would never play you for a fool."

He held up a hand to stop her when she opened

her mouth to protest. "Yes, from the first day you arrived Gus tried to bully me into 'sweet-talking' you on the town's behalf. But I flat-out told him—over and over again—that I wouldn't do it. I think you'll have to agree that from the moment we first re-met at Kit's there was no sweet-talking to win your favor."

Her lip curled. "Changed your mind pretty quick, though, didn't you?"

"I didn't. And I haven't."

"Oh, right. What about the grand tour of Canyon Springs the two of you set up? The flower delivery and the attempted dinner at Hector's? And don't forget Friday night. You—"

Something flickered through his eyes, jerking her tirade to a halt.

"Friday night." His words came softly as he stepped even closer, his intent gaze now lingering on her lips. "You mean when you thought I wanted to do this?"

Before she could object, he gently slipped his hand under her hair and behind her neck, leaning in to capture her mouth with his.

Stunned, it was all she could do to remain standing as his lips tenderly caressed hers. His familiar scent, the warm touch, sent fiery memories rebounding through her now-muddled mind. Laughter and longing. Starry nights and dreams of a lifetime shared. The certainty she was right where God wanted her to be.

With a sigh of surrender, she slipped her arms around his neck and drew him closer.

To Jake's pleased surprise, Macy melted into the warmth of his arms and returned his kiss. Encouraged, he permitted himself to take pleasure in this rare, sweet moment of holding her. Drinking in her citrusy scent. Savoring her softness, the taste of her lips. This was the woman he'd once believed God had given him for a lifetime. Things had gone wrong. But now she was back in his life. In his arms. Could God be giving him the go-ahead?

He slowly drew back to look into her eyes. "I've missed you."

"I've…missed you, too."

He grazed his lips along hers once more, then drew a calming breath. "Macy, I'd never play the mayor's game with anyone—but I definitely wouldn't play it with you. I don't care what he thinks or what he says, I'm telling the truth. Can you believe that?"

Without hesitation she nodded, her luminous, now-trusting gaze fixed on his.

Relief washed through him as his fingertips caressed the softness of her jawline. "Thank you for believing me."

They stood in silence for several long moments, then, despite his somewhat sweaty state, Macy snuggled in closer to press the side of her face against his chest as if reluctant to let him go. "I'm sorry, Jake. For so many things."

As was he. Six lost years.

She pulled back to look at him uncertainly. "I was wrong. So wrong to have written that story without consulting you. I could say I was young. Stupid. Selfish. But—"

"And no doubt influenced by your mother."

She hung her head, no longer able to face him. "I can't blame her. It was my doing. Can you forgive me?"

He slipped his hand under her chin and raised it so he could look into her beautiful eyes. "I already have. Long ago."

A doubtful smile tugged at her lips. "From the welcome you gave me my first day here, you could have fooled me."

"I'd forgiven you for the past. But I admit I wasn't inclined to permit a repeat performance."

"I'm sorry I hurt you. And your friend." She took his hands in hers and gazed up at him. "I didn't consciously set out to do that. But I can see now that I let my personal feelings, my resentment, guide my actions rather than God."

"Your resentment? Toward me, you mean?"

Her hands tightened on his. "We'd been seeing each other for months, hadn't we? Spending our free time together. Growing close. Or so I thought. But you—" She halted as if doubting the wisdom of continuing. Of sharing her thoughts.

"But I what?"

She garnered her courage to continue. "We were

obviously more than friends—or so the kisses implied. You'd taken up every spare minute of my time since that first weekend in October. By springtime graduation was looming, yet you never gave any indication of how you felt about me. Not a hint beyond the kisses, that is. I knew how little those could mean from previous romantic involvements."

His throat suddenly went dry. He couldn't believe his ears. She'd thought he was using her? That their kisses meant nothing to him?

"How could you not know," he asked, his voice husky, "how I felt about you?"

"You never talked about us having a future together. You never said you…loved me. How was I to know you cared for me more than just as a friend?"

"But I…" His mind raced back in time. "You thought I kissed every woman I met? I picked you up for church every week, didn't I? I always got you there early because you didn't like walking in late. I bought you a Sunday paper because you enjoyed a hard copy. I never failed to meet you after your night classes so you wouldn't walk home alone in the dark. I took you for drives to the little towns you loved. And I…" What else? He'd done a ton of stuff. "I kept your car's tires inflated."

Her eyes widened. "You did what?"

"Every week I checked your tire pressure." He offered an emphatic nod. "Faithfully."

Her pretty mouth all but gaping, she shook her

head in disbelief. "I don't know whether to laugh or cry."

He frowned, not understanding her response at all. "Why would you do either?"

"Jake!" She reached up to place her hands on either side of his face. "Most women want to hear the words, but you were checking my tires?"

"You caught me doing it." He shot her an indignant look. "Don't pretend you didn't know."

Her hands slid down to lay flat on his chest. "I thought it was a quirky habit. An eccentricity."

"I wanted to make sure you didn't wear the tread down unevenly. Or have a flat someplace where you'd be left vulnerable, like on your drives to see your folks in St. Louis."

She stared up at him, her eyes searching his for the longest moment. A tiny smile touched her lips. "You nut."

With a laugh, she threw her arms around his neck.

Startled, he nevertheless joined in the embrace, relishing the warmth of her cuddling into his arms. When they finally drew apart, he lifted her chin with his finger. "You know, now that I think about it, why am I the only one getting beat up for not using the *L* word? You never said it either."

"Because I'm old-fashioned." She ducked her head. "I thought that was for you to say first."

"Oh, you did, did you?" In about two seconds he was going to kiss that prudish look right off her face.

But before he could make a move, the glare of car

lights spotlighted them on the deck. A horn blared as a vehicle made its way down the dirt drive. Heart pounding, he cast a resentful look in the intruder's direction as he and Macy broke apart.

The vehicle came to a halt. The engine cut off. Then the lights. A door creaked open, slammed. A tall, shadowy form made its way toward them.

"Now that's what I like to see," a familiar voice called out.

The mayor of Canyon Springs.

Chapter Sixteen

"Are you sure, Ava?"

Excitement rising at Ava's early-morning disclosure, Macy leaned back in the window seat of her room at Nancy's B and B, where she'd been reliving the unexpected events of the previous night. Talk about poor timing on the mayor's part. He'd claimed to have city council business to discuss with Jake, so she'd immediately slipped away. Would she hear from Jake today?

"One hundred percent sure." Ava's voice held a note of satisfaction. "You were right. I compared the photo of your Dexter from the museum article to the photo of Tommy O'Donner. Your Dexter's online obituary didn't include a photograph, but I agree the O'Donner in my photo is the Dexter in yours."

Macy struggled to wrap her mind around the facts. "So the identifying caption got switched? The records made a mistake? Dexter didn't die in 1941?"

"No, Dexter did die…." Ava paused almost dramatically. "I've done some more digging. Your Dexter *is* Tommy O'Donner."

"What?" Macy rose to her feet.

"I think Tommy took his friend's name—and other personal information like his birth date—after his friend was killed at Pearl Harbor."

"Wait, wait, wait. My head's spinning." Not only from Jake's kisses last night, but from the discovery her friend had presented her with. She paced the floor. "You're saying my Dexter wasn't Dexter at all? He was this O'Donner guy? He stole his friend's identity? Why would he do that?"

"I've found proof Tommy was shipped home from Hawaii after the attack with severe injuries. As well as I can piece together, he had a long recovery, then moved to Chicago to take a bookkeeping job."

"He had to steal his friend's identity to do that?"

"No, as far as I can tell he was using his own name then. The switch happened later after he testified against his employers—kingpins in organized crime."

Macy halted. "He betrayed mobsters?"

He was either crazy or courageous.

"He probably figured he'd soon be a dead man anyway if he didn't come forward. According to the Chicago papers, a coworker had been snuffed out the previous year. Tommy's testimony was instrumental in putting the murderers behind bars."

"And then what happened?"

"And then—" The lilt in her tone clued Macy in that Ava was enjoying toying with her.

"Come on, Ava."

"He disappeared."

"And came to Canyon Springs as Dexter Smith," she concluded, finally catching on.

"That's what I'm guessing," her friend confirmed. "How it came about is anybody's guess. I don't imagine there was a formal witness protection program in the 1940s. But that doesn't mean someone didn't step in to make sure he had appropriate documentation to make a clean getaway."

"Someone made certain a former soldier who'd served his country got a fresh start."

"Speculation, but that's what it looks like. We know for a fact that O'Donner is the Dexter Smith in Canyon Springs. I'll send you the link to the papers and the trial photos."

"From what I saw at the Canyon Springs museum, this pseudo Dexter arrived here as a successful businessman. Since he grew up in an orphanage and had no family support, he must have been given a substantial nest egg for relocation."

Ava chuckled. "Not necessarily. From what the papers say, he was aware all along of who his employers were. I'm inclined to think our business-savvy bookkeeper filled his pockets on the side. Embezzled from the mob."

"Wow." Mind racing, Macy lowered herself to the bed. "You know what this means, don't you?"

"I sure do. You've got yourself a story, sweetie. Canyon Springs is indebted to a man with mob ties."

Jake hunched over the papers on his office desk, hoping he looked intent on resolving a legal problem should Phyllis Diane or a colleague knock at the door. But that was far from the truth. While Gus hadn't left until late the previous night and Jake had hardly slept at all, this morning his mind was alert and focused, although not on the documents spread out before him. He'd come to the office before dawn, knowing it was too early to call Macy, and had spent the time in prayer.

After too many lonely years, he'd held Macy Colston in his arms. Tasted the sweetness of her lips and found himself thinking about a life shared with her. But while holding her seemed so right, while past misunderstandings had been aired out, there were still things between them that weren't easily fixed.

He glanced over at the beagle curled up on the rug by a filing cabinet. "Macy has her heart set on a high profile career. The blog. Books. Maybe a television show."

Abe whimpered and rose to his feet, tail wagging.

"Yeah, well that's easy for you to say. But the woman I love—" there, he'd admitted to the word "—has her heart set on a dream that puts her on the road most of the year. Macy's a city gal, too. What can I offer to keep her in Canyon Springs with me?"

Abe trotted up to him, toenails clicking on the hardwood floor, soulful eyes appearing to offer sympathy.

"What? You think I shouldn't expect her to? That I should be the one to make changes in my own life? Go with her on her town-to-town journeys?"

He'd prayed about the situation most of the night, trying to find a way for it to work between them. But he had commitments here. People depended on him, both Grandma and his clients. He couldn't leave them in a lurch. And what about *his* dreams? To become mayor. A state representative. Wasn't that the direction God had been leading him?

He glanced at the photo of his Grandma and Granddad. What would they advise? Married for sixty-five years, their life had impacted his own in untold ways. While his mother and father's marriage hadn't provided any assurance that love lasted, Ginny and Dexter's had given him hope in the darkest hours of his own love life disappointments.

He straightened in his chair, his heart suddenly lightening as a sense of peace and firm direction filled him. Grandma had arrived in town unexpectedly on the bus yesterday, calling Jake to pick her up at the Main Street stop and claiming she'd had enough with being referee to Jake's sister's kids.

He glanced down at Abe. "What do you say I take Macy to meet Grandma? Let her hear firsthand what it's like to spend a lifetime in Canyon Springs with a man you love."

* * *

Macy logged on to her email to pull up the documents Ava had forwarded, then glanced at the clock. Nine-thirty. Surely Jake would call, wouldn't he?

Eagerly perusing the electronic documents, she still couldn't believe what she was seeing. Tommy O'Donner. Dexter Smith. Chicago mob affiliations that led to one of Canyon Springs's prominent citizens.

Wow. As soon as she went through all the attachments with a fine-toothed comb, she'd start writing. With only a few days remaining in her visit to Canyon Springs, the timing of this couldn't be any better.

"Thank You, Lord," she whispered, gratefulness welling in her heart. She'd always heard God was never late but that He was also seldom early, which sure seemed to be the case this time. She pulled out her phone, eager to share the good news with her family. Maybe they'd listen next time she told them to keep the faith, to trust her.

"Hey, Mom. How goes it?"

Not picking up on the enthusiastic tone of her daughter, Trina Colston immediately launched in on her. "I checked your blog this morning, Macy. What's the holdup on that promised story? From the sound of your posts, you're having a wonderful time at this assignment, but too often you've forfeited opportunities. Good reporting means asking hard questions, making people uncomfortable."

Confident in Ava's research, her mother's words

bounced off her without a dent. She couldn't suppress a smile. "Relax, Mom. I now have a story that will bring the whole town up short."

Dead silence.

"Oh?"

She could tell from her mother's tone she hadn't anticipated her daughter would have anything more to offer than excuses.

"I have research to wrap up, but this story has the punch I've been holding out for. You're not going to believe it but—"

An inner impression halted her, a warning not to share what she was about to share. But why not? It would get her mother off her back, wouldn't it? Mom might have ideas on how to frame it for the blog. Whether she should drop a few hints throughout the rest of the week to build suspense or lay it all on the line her final day in Canyon Springs.

She rose from her desk chair and moved to the window, but the inner impression didn't evaporate. If anything, it was even stronger. *Don't say anything more.*

"I won't believe what?" her mother prompted.

"That…you're going to have to wait until I post it. Just like the rest of the world."

"Macy, don't do this to me." Her mother's tone was sharp, reprimanding—and much too familiar.

"I want it to be a surprise." She cringed as the words left her mouth. Her mother hated surprises.

"How delightful," her mother mocked. "But the truth of it is you don't have a story yet, do you?"

The accusatory words pierced. "I do. But I'm not ready to share it."

"Because you don't think it will pass muster. That's why, isn't it?"

"I think it will, Mom. But I have to make sure I have my facts straight." *Make sure Jake's okay with it.*

Jake? Where did that come from?

From the silence on the other end of the line, it was evident her mother still didn't believe she had a story.

But she did. And it was a good one. One that would prove to her mother once and for all that Macy knew what she was doing.

"Trust me, Mom."

"I want to trust you, sweetheart, but you don't know how quickly opportunities can slip through your fingers. When I was your age…"

She drifted off into a rerun of the past. When the tale finally wound down, further embellished with each telling, Macy quickly reassured her and said her goodbyes.

Between her mother's response and the realization she needed to engage Jake in the shaping of the blog post, the excitement at her story "find" deflated. She returned to the desk and sat down.

Of course she had to tell Jake. No more surprises like the last time. But what if he nixed the story altogether? Said it would harm Dexter-Tommy's descendants in the community? That it would shame the town to have it publicized that someone with mob connections had helped build the Canyon Springs they loved?

If she didn't post it, she'd lose her sponsor for sure. And her family's approval and support. And what would she have in its place?

Her memory shifted to the previous night. Jake had claimed he'd cared for her in the past, that he'd proven it over and over by the things he'd done for her.

He said he'd forgiven her.

But this morning she'd realized there had been no words of love. Words of commitment. Granted, the mayor's arrival and his hearty pleasure in finding them in each other's arms had changed the evening's atmosphere.

Did Jake love her? Love her enough to want to spend his life with her? She knew she loved him, but that didn't change their circumstances. He was wedded to this small town and she had big dreams waiting over the horizon. Dreams that stood a strong chance of coming to fruition if the posting of the Dexter-Tommy story satisfied her sponsor.

Perhaps it would be easier to post the story and ask Jake's forgiveness later rather than for his permission now to do so. Surely, once he understood the immensity of the opportunity awaiting her, he'd understand how an event that took place almost seventy years ago was fair game.

Could she take that risk?

* * *

Macy stared down at the text message on her phone.

My grandma's invited us to lunch today. If I don't hear from you to the contrary, I'll pick you up at the B and B at eleven-thirty.

Grandma? He wanted her to meet his grandmother? Did he need her approval before he'd be ready to address the future of their relationship? She glanced at her watch. Almost eleven. That didn't give her much time to make herself presentable. She moved toward the closet. Halted. Turned in the direction of the bathroom. Stopped again.

He wanted her to meet his grandma.

That had to be a good indication of how he felt about her, didn't it? She knew how much he valued his grandparents. But shouldn't they get a few things resolved between them first, before he started introducing her to the family?

Nevertheless, she took a deep breath and texted back. See you soon. Then dashed for the closet.

Forty-five minutes later Jake escorted her up the sidewalk to his grandma's place, looking forward to this visit if his bright-eyed gaze was any indication.

"I know I said it on the way over, but you look beautiful today, Macy."

"Thank you." She'd changed clothes twice, freshened her makeup, then switched to the turquoise sheath and sweater she'd worn on her first visit to

Canyon Springs Christian Church. Dressy, but not formal. Goodness knows she needed the added assurance of feeling comfortable when she met his grandma.

What had he told his grandmother about her that elicited the invitation to lunch? That they'd known each other before? Had broken up years ago and now they were…what? She wished she'd asked Jake on the ride over, but she'd been too nervous to think straight.

She placed a hand on his arm. "Jake, what's your grandmother's name?"

"Virginia. But everyone calls her Ginny."

"And what did you—"

But she was cut off as the screen door to the attractively landscaped ranch house opened before they'd even started up the steps. A smiling, fair-haired woman dressed in dark slacks and a pullover top stepped out to welcome them. Her eyes were Jake's eyes—that same clear, alert blue with laugh lines radiating from the corners. She took Macy's hands in hers.

"So this is Macy." She cut a teasing glance at Jake. What had he told her? Then her eyes smiled warmly into those of his guest. "I'm Ginny. And I'm delighted to meet you, my dear, even if it is *six years* after my grandson first laid eyes on you."

The older woman eyed Jake and shook her head.

He looked a bit sheepish. "Yeah, well, better late than never, Gran."

"True. Now please come in. I know Jake has limited time for lunch breaks on weekdays, so we have only to put the food on the table."

Macy followed his grandmother inside as she led them through a sunny living room and into the adjoining dining room. His grandma gestured for them to sit down at the oval table, where a cherry red tablecloth with floral cloth napkins lent a cheerful touch. A graceful glass swan filled with shiny Granny Smith apples served as a homey centerpiece.

"I'll have everything out here in a minute."

"I can help, Gran." Jake motioned Macy to make herself at home before following his grandma to the kitchen. His low, rumbling voice came clearly from the other room. "I told you she was pretty, didn't I?"

She couldn't catch Ginny's whispered response, but things seemed to be off to a good start. She gazed around the room, immediately drawn to a lovely antique buffet, its simple lines complementing the uncluttered decor. Atop it was a lineup of family photos and Macy eagerly moved in for closer inspection.

Oh, my goodness. That had to be Jake when he was a toddler. His tiny face wore the same solemn look of concentration that often colored his grown-up features. One hand gripped that of a pretty young woman in a denim skirt and tank top. His mother?

Smiling, Macy moved along the photos of Jake and those she supposed to be his little sister and half brother. In his high school graduation photo, the cap-and-gowned Jake was clearly recognizable, yet only a shadow of who he was today.

"I keep telling Gran to put those in the attic." Macy detected a groan in Jake's voice as he placed a bread basket and a platter of deli meats on the table, then joined her at the buffet.

"You were such a handsome little guy." She pointed at the chubby-legged toddler and Jake bumped her with his elbow.

"What do you mean *were?*" The expression on his face as he studied his childhood self was identical to that in the photograph.

"Using past tense doesn't negate the present, Mr. Talford."

"That's better." With a satisfied nod, he again disappeared into the kitchen only to reappear with a lazy Susan of condiments and a bowl of fresh strawberries.

"Is this your dad?"

He moved to her side, his expression grim. "That's him."

"I can see a strong resemblance. The height and build. Your nose. The crooked smile. But I knew immediately you have your grandmother's eyes."

"So I've been told. Except for that, I guess my dad's genes dominated. I don't look a thing like my granddad."

She searched the photos. "Is there one of him here?"

"Right there." He pointed to the far wall, cast in shadow from sunlight streaming through the windows.

She approached for a closer look, Jake right behind her. He placed his hands at her waist, a reassuring gesture.

"No resemblance at all, do you think?"

But Macy couldn't respond. She could only lean against Jake as her legs threatened to give way. The black-and-white portrait showed a still-identifiable young Ginny and her husband. A suited man, one eye twinkling mischievously at the camera. The other remained closed, obliterated by scar tissue.

Dexter Smith.

Tommy O'Donner.

Chapter Seventeen

"That's our wedding portrait, January 1947," Grandma supplied as she carried a bowl of green beans into the dining room. "Dexter insisted we have one."

"I was telling Macy," Jake said, enjoying the feeling of Macy leaning back against his chest as if she could count on him to be there for her, "that I don't resemble Granddad. But she noticed I have your eyes."

"As do your sister and mother," Grandma confirmed. "The two of them have a stronger resemblance to the maternal side of the family, but you inherited your father's looks."

"Fortunately not his ethics." Had Dad ever made a promise he hadn't broken?

"You got those from your mother's side, that's a fact." Gran motioned to the table. "Have a seat, you two."

He glanced at Macy, who'd remained uncharacteristically quiet, studying the portrait of his grandparents. Was she thinking about all those years they'd spent living in Canyon Springs? About what a future with him might offer for the next fifty years?

The prospect warmed him. He took Macy's hand, surprisingly icy in his grasp, to turn her toward the table. Her coloring appeared ashen. Was she coming down with something? Concerned, he guided her to a chair, then took the one next to her.

"Would you like to say grace, Jake?" His grandma had already bowed her head. Macy did likewise.

He cleared his throat. "Father God, we thank You for this time together. For the food Grandma's prepared and that Macy can be here to share it with us. I especially thank You for Grandma and Granddad, and for the influence their love for each other has had on my life. For the example they've set for living in a way that is pleasing to You. In Your son's name…"

"Amen" echoed around the table.

"Help yourself to whatever's here." Gran pushed the beans toward Jake, then turned to Macy. "I apologize that there's nothing much made from scratch on the table. I just returned from a visit to Phoenix and haven't settled back in yet."

"No apologies necessary." Macy managed a smile, though not with its usual wattage. "It looks and smells delicious."

"I'm sure the local ladies have fed you much better during your stay here." Gran leaned forward. "So I'll let you off the hook and won't expect you to feature our lunch in tomorrow's blog."

When they'd served themselves, Macy bit into the green beans, closing her eyes momentarily, apparently savoring the taste. "Despite your disclaimer, I absolutely must have this recipe, Ginny. I've never been a big fan of green beans, but these are amazing. I'd never have thought to add pecans."

Grandma beamed. "I saw it on one of those big name chef cooking shows. Then tweaked it a bit."

Conscious of the limited time for lunch, Jake nodded toward his grandparents' wedding portrait. "So, Grandma, you and Granddad were married sixty-five years. That's quite a record."

Her eyes smiled knowingly into his. Of course she'd figure out what he was up to. "We had our challenges, but they were good years that sped by too quickly."

Macy nodded, her expression sympathetic. "I understand he passed away not too long ago?"

Jake tensed. How'd she know that? She must have been snooping around at the historical museum or pumping locals for insider information. Then it hit him. Oh, yeah, he'd told her about Granddad that day he'd run into her at the museum. But the false alarm reminded him they still had things to work out—trust issues between them.

Grandma smiled at Macy. "We lost him last summer."

"I'm sorry. How did the two of you meet, if you don't mind me asking?"

Gran's voice warmed. "My father worked for the railroad in Winslow when I saw Dexter Smith step off the train. March 1946."

"Love at first sight?" Macy prompted, a smile in her voice, but her coloring still didn't look good.

"For me it was." Grandma reached for a bread slice. "I don't think he even saw me and I was too shy to come forward. But I did overhear him asking someone how to get to Zane Grey country. I guess he'd read Mr. Grey's books and after a long train trip across the somewhat barren Southwest he was more than ready to experience ponderosa pine country."

Grandma forked a piece of deli turkey onto her mayo-slathered bread. "Then a few months later when I graduated from high school, I saw an advertisement in the paper. Someone in Canyon Springs was looking for office assistance. I'd taken typing, bookkeeping and filing classes in school, so I hitched a ride here." Grandma cast Macy a warning glance. "It was safer in those days, dear. Don't try that now."

Macy set her fork on the edge of her plate and leaned forward. "So then what happened?"

"The business looking for office help happened to be owned by Jake's grandfather."

Grandma seemed to be enjoying talking about her husband. He'd have to thank Macy later for her interest.

"His business must have already been turning a profit if he was hiring help."

Macy studied Grandma intently as she often did

when pursuing a story. He'd have to get used to that again, to how she sometimes interrogated people even in casual conversation.

"He was a diligent saver, but he'd also come into some money once he reached his majority. His parents were apparently rather well off."

"You don't know for certain?"

"They died when he was small, so he didn't know much about them himself. He was raised in an orphanage."

"Where?"

Grandma looked slightly taken aback as Macy fired off the question and he stepped in. "Near Chicago."

He passed a small bowl of carrot sticks to Macy, but she set it on the table. "So he came here on his own after World War II. Had he been in the service?"

"No. He sustained injuries when he was younger that prevented him from active military duty. I'm sure you noticed the more obvious one in our photograph."

"The loss of his eye."

Grandma nodded.

"But he loved his country," Jake inserted, again picking up the carrot sticks and handing them to Macy. She placed them back on the table, her gaze never leaving his grandma's face. He should have warned Gran how Macy could be terrier-like when a story caught her attention. How could he steer this conversation around to sixty-five happy years in small-town America?

"As Grandma said, they faced lots of challenges through the years, but shared a lifetime of love. Right, Gran?"

His grandmother smiled at him, detecting his strategic attempt to change the subject. Macy, her forehead still creased and deep in thought, refocused on her lunch, finally helping herself to the carrot sticks.

"He seldom talked about it, Macy," Gran continued, "but it was evident Dex's growing up years were rough. He had little reason to believe a heavenly Father looked out for him. But the glue that kept us together was that when he'd come to Canyon Springs, he spent long stretches of time alone in the great outdoors asking himself and his Creator hard questions. Not long before we were engaged, he turned his life over to God."

Jake pushed back his now-empty plate and dished up a bowl of fresh strawberries. "Granddad always said you were the first and best gift God gave him after he made that life-changing decision."

"That sentiment was mutual. We were two very different, very imperfect people who together matured spiritually through the years. That's what made the difference. Our willingness to let God play an active role in our relationship."

Jake glanced at Macy, who remained silent, her gaze once again trained thoughtfully on his grandma. Was she taking this in?

Their own future didn't look promising if her troubled expression was any indication. He'd thought talking to Grandma, hearing of a lasting marriage between two diverse people, would encourage her, lay a foundation before he shared specific words of love or made suggestions as to how they could build a life together.

He'd coasted around saying he loved her last night. He alluded to it, but hadn't said it. Gus barging in had something to do with it, but to his way of thinking you didn't say the words unless you were committed—and had a ring in your back pocket.

Which he did.

He'd dug it out of a dresser drawer when the mayor finally left last night. As he'd held the ring in his hand, he marveled anew that he'd kept it. It wasn't as if he would have ever given it to anyone else. No one would want a symbol of his love for another woman.

Jake glanced again at Macy, the conversation having turned to the unseasonably warm weather in her hometown of St. Louis.

Am I getting ahead of myself, Lord?

His heart nearly exploded from his chest every time he looked at her. How had he lived without her in his life? Having Macy in town these few short weeks left him realizing he didn't want to face a future without her in it.

But was that what God wanted?

She glanced at him, her eyes questioning. Curious at his silence?

Then he smiled. He couldn't help himself.

She smiled back.

His heart swelled with certainty. Yes, this is what he wanted and he had a feeling both Macy and God wanted it, too.

That had been the longest ninety minutes of her life.

Macy's stomach continued on a roller-coaster ride even hours after Jake dropped her off at Dix's Woodland Warehouse for her afternoon assignment. She couldn't believe Dexter Smith—or rather Tommy O'Donner—was Jake's maternal grandfather.

The thought still made her queasy as she attempted to focus on unpacking a box of canned fruit. Despite her journalistic instincts, she hadn't had a clue when studying Dexter-Tommy's photos that there was any connection to Jake. As had been confirmed today, he looked nothing like his ancestor.

It was a wonder she hadn't passed out when she saw Ginny and Dexter's wedding portrait. She'd felt light-headed and might have collapsed if it hadn't been for the support of Jake's sturdy frame behind her.

How can this be happening, Lord?

Dexter Smith's story was her ticket to the future. The admission price to winning her family's approval once and for all. She thought God was working with her on this, that He'd found her a story that happened so long ago that the events, while perhaps shocking in retrospect, held little present-day sting—a juicy exposé that wouldn't leave anyone feeling truly hurt.

"I know we're limited on shelf space as we stock up for the busy season—" Sharon Dixon's amused voice rang out behind her. "But I think we can find a spot for that canned fruit besides a freezer unit."

Jerked from her reverie, Macy stared at the glass door beside her and laughed. Sure enough, there sat half a dozen cans, right next to the ice cream. "Oh, dear. Good thing you caught me, Sharon, or those would have been ruined for sure."

"Have something weighing on your mind, doll?"

Macy opened the freezer and retrieved the fruit, then secured the door once again. Sharon was easy to talk to, yet she couldn't share details of her predicament. But maybe generalities? Sharon might have some insights.

Macy carefully shelved the cans, then reached into the box for another. "Actually…have you ever found yourself in a situation where the first time you made a decision you were blind to the ramifications? Unintentionally hurt someone? And then a similar situation later arises, with the risk of hurting the same someone you'd hurt before?"

Sharon studied her thoughtfully. "Are you by any chance talking about Jake Talford?"

Macy's hands tightened on the can. Had the mayor stumbling upon them in an intimate moment last night already made its way through the Canyon Springs grapevine?

Sharon nodded knowingly. "You're the little gal who broke his heart back in Missouri, aren't you?"

Macy's heart jolted as she self-consciously turned to place the can on the shelf. Had she broken his heart? Or merely made him angry? "What makes you think that?"

"I sensed a familiarity between you two when he was here the other day." She handed two more cans to Macy. "When he came back to Canyon Springs for Christmas after his first semester of grad school, I could tell there was something different about him. A buoyancy. A happiness."

"That would tend to catch your attention," Macy acknowledged. "He's often so serious."

A sad smile touched Sharon's lips. "Try having your dad walk out of your life when you're in second grade and having to step up to see to your mother and sister's welfare when your stepdad isn't much more dependable than your father. Things of that nature change a kid. Put too much responsibility on his shoulders."

"Did he...tell anyone about me?"

Sharon shook her head. "Not that I know of, unless he told his grandparents. But I'd known him since he was a kid so it didn't take a lot of effort to figure out he'd found the woman of his dreams. No doubt about it, he was crazy in love that Christmas. But it was a different story when he moved here later the next summer."

Had her betrayal sent him retreating to Canyon

Springs? "I made a professional decision he didn't agree with."

"So things are working out between you once more," Sharon summarized. "But another professional decision stands in the way?"

"My blog's growing popularity is bringing incredible career opportunities. Continued travel. Books. Maybe a television program."

Sharon gave a low whistle. "That *is* an opportunity."

"It's huge. A dream come true. But there's something I need to do to make it happen. And it's not something that can sit on hold indefinitely."

"You have to make a decision that may again hurt Jake."

"I think so." No, she *knew* so.

"Will it hurt you if you make the choice that spares Jake?"

"If I say no to the opportunity, it will close the door on an exciting and lucrative career path—one I've sacrificed time, energy, creativity and even a personal life for." Macy shelved the fruit, then turned again to Sharon. "So, yes, if I close the door it will hurt. Deeply disappoint. Not only me, but others who are counting on me."

"And yet...?"

"Saying no to it holds no guarantees that—" Macy gave Sharon a frank look "—well, that there will be a future with Jake."

Both were silent for a long moment, then Sharon

handed her one last can. "You do have a decision on your hands. I can see why the fruit ended up in the freezer." Sharon offered an understanding smile, endeavoring to lighten the moment.

"I've prayed for so long that doors like this would open for my career. I thought God was working with me, had possibly found a way to—"

"Have your cake and eat it, too?"

"That's what I hoped anyway, until a short time ago when an unexpected twist came out of nowhere. It changes everything I'd been certain of. If I take the steps necessary to ensure an invitation into this new endeavor, Jake will never forgive me."

"You can't be sure of that, doll. You should talk to him. Come to a decision together since it affects the future of both of you."

Sharon made it sound so simple.

"I'm afraid," Macy said, shelving the final can as the truth about Jake's grandfather weighed heavily, "that I already know what his decision will be."

Chapter Eighteen

Lunch at Grandma's hadn't quite turned out as Jake had hoped. Macy had seemed preoccupied, distracted. Except for when she was questioning Grandma. For that, she was oddly intent. Which might be only natural. It wasn't every day he took a woman home to meet Grandma and she likely knew it. Maybe she'd just been nervous, trying too hard to show interest in Grandma's life. He only hoped the time there had given her some food for thought.

Still energized from the kisses of the previous evening, Jake stepped out the back door of his place after work, then crouched down to roughhouse a few minutes with an ecstatic Abe.

In a phone conversation with Grandma that afternoon, she'd seemed elated with Macy. Beautiful girl. Bright. Charming. Oh, and inquisitive, as well. That would take getting used to. But what, she'd accused, had he been thinking to let her get away from him in the first place?

Of course, he hadn't shared the details of that earlier time with Grandma. Having forgiven Macy for her youthful betrayal, he had no business sharing it with anyone now. So how much longer, Grandma had demanded to know, would Macy be in town? When would they be returning to share another meal? And surely he didn't intend to let her slip away from him again?

The beagle rolled over on his back for a belly rub and Jake accommodated him. "It's not as easy as Grandma thinks, is it, fella?"

That was one of his shortcomings. He always needed to have everything figured out in advance. Mapped out in detail. He had to see a situation from all angles and anticipate any challenges. Loopholes. Potholes. Deal breakers. And then he took steps to ensure he had a counter move to nip negative repercussions in the bud. While that made him a good lawyer, it sure wreaked havoc with a man's love life.

But a plan was formulating…one that was actually pretty spontaneous. For him anyway, if "plans" could ever be considered "spontaneous."

Surely she couldn't have mistaken his intentions when he'd kissed her last night before the mayor intruded? They hadn't had a chance to discuss it further, but he was acutely aware that, just as she'd pointed out, he'd never told her he loved her. He still hadn't told her.

She said she was old-fashioned, that she thought he was supposed to say it first.

"It sure would have been a lot easier on me if she'd been the one to speak up, Abe. Why's it always up to the guy? Why are we supposed to be the ones to go out on a limb?"

Years ago he'd turned himself inside out trying to discern how she felt about him. He'd thought at the time an answer to that question would be a starter as to how God might feel about it. But even when he'd been beginning to get a clue, he'd used the excuse that he'd had one too many disappointments in his past and needed to be cautious. Certain. He didn't want to end up like his mom and dad. So he'd dragged his feet on telling her how he felt about her, convincing himself she'd probably heard guys use those special words for their own selfish purposes without a promise for the future.

But a ring. That would confirm the value of his words. And that's what he'd acquired.

Only it had been too late.

He smiled to himself as a tingle of anticipation raced through him. It wasn't going to be too late this time.

All signs pointed to her feeling the same way about him as he did her, that God was giving the go-ahead. Macy only had a few more days left in Canyon Springs, so what was he waiting for?

He glanced at his watch. Five-thirty. Giving Abe a final hearty pat, he stood.

"So what do you say I hit the florist before she

closes at six? I think this mission calls for a dozen roses, don't you?"

The dog looked at him curiously, tail wagging.

"Oh, yeah, I promise to come back and get cleaned up. I'd better dust off that ring, too."

What should she do now?

Macy stared at the papers spread on the bed, desktop and window seat. She'd printed them on her portable printer as soon as she'd gotten back to her room and received additional emails with attachments from Ava.

Despite desperation for a suitable story, she'd hoped there might have been a mistake, that old newspapers had erroneously reported on the situation. But there was no doubt Dexter and Tommy were one and the same and Tommy had had connections to the 1940s Chicago underworld.

She picked up one of the printouts and read again the headlines that splashed the crime bosses' convictions across the front page. In slightly smaller print below, it confirmed Tommy's testimony played a major part in closing the case. Amazing how a newspaper printed things like that with an identifying photo, for all intents and purposes placing a target on young Tommy's back.

Then again, he may have served his country and served it well, bore the visible wounds of that commitment, but he'd made some bad decisions. Choices that would haunt him until the day he departed this world.

How much of his disreputable history had he told his wife? Had they together concocted a whitewash of his past? Lies such as the one that he'd been injured as a youth, not in combat. That he'd received an inheritance that explained his moneyed arrival in Canyon Springs. Obviously Ginny was aware of bits and pieces of truth from his past, such as his being an orphan.

But the biggest question of all was did *Jake* know the truth?

She'd broken a cardinal rule of journalism today, assuming neither he nor his grandmother knew of the Dexter Smith-Tommy O'Donner connection.

What if Jake had known all along? What if, as he'd claimed, his romantic attentions toward her had nothing to do with the mayor's prodding but were, instead, intended to keep a finger on the pulse of her blog? To develop a superficial bridge between them, knowing a renewed relationship might prevent her from uncovering the truth and then shouting Dexter-Tommy's misdeeds from the blogging rooftop?

Jake hadn't told her he loved her last night. Had introducing her to his grandmother today been a ploy to reinforce her loyalty? To buy her complicity in keeping the family secret?

Had she been the one betrayed this time?

Shaken, Macy seated herself at the desk and opened her laptop, preparing to weave final facts into a drafted post. Maybe that would help her think more clearly. Putting things down in words often did.

She'd barely begun when a knock came at the door.

Nancy must be bringing a plate of those tasty molasses cookies as she often did in the evenings. But when Macy opened the door, she gasped.

There stood Jake with a vase of red roses. And scattered all over the room behind her lay evidence of his grandfather's unsavory past.

"Good evening, Macy." His eyes smiled into hers as he held out the flowers. "May I come in?"

Come in? He couldn't come in.

"I'm…in the middle of a deadline."

"Oh." A wavering in his eyes communicated disappointment that a visit from him, bearing flowers, didn't rate higher than a deadline. "It won't take long."

What choice did she have? But she'd keep him corralled just inside the door.

She offered the smile she'd been too shocked to share when she'd found him on her doorstep. Reaching out to accept the roses, she then stepped back to allow him passage. Once inside, he pushed the door closed.

What did he have to say to her that required such privacy?

The expression in his eyes was like that of a little boy hoping to please, and she was reminded of the photos of him lining his grandmother's buffet top.

"These are beautiful, Jake. Thank you." There, she'd remembered her manners.

"Have you eaten yet? It's a bit of a drive, but I

thought we might go to Show Low for dinner. Or take a walk if you'd prefer. We could stroll down to Camilla's for takeout and have ourselves a picnic."

She set the vase on a small table near the door. "It will be dark soon."

His eyes twinkled. "I have a flashlight."

Jake being spontaneous was a new twist. That wasn't something he'd been known for. He was a planner, a ducks in a row kind of guy. But a walk would get him out of her room.

"A picnic sounds wonderful."

"Then get your sweater. It will cool down quickly after the sun sets."

Smiling, she kept her eyes riveted on him as she backed away, hoping to keep his attention on her and off the rest of the room. Standing sideways at the closet door, she reached in only to find the hanger empty. Now where had her sweater gotten off to?

"There it is." Jake moved toward her desk before she could cut him off. He snagged her sweater from the back of the chair and held it out so she had only to slip her arms into the sleeves. Holding her breath, she stepped toward him and he helped her on with it.

"It looks as if you have a big project underway." He gestured to the bed and desk covered with neatly organized stacks of printer paper.

"A little research."

Curiosity lit his eyes. "For the blog? On Canyon Springs?"

"Um, some of it is."

"Mind if I look?"

Oh, no.

"Why should I mind?" She slipped her arm in the crook of his. "But I think I'd like to go for that promised walk to Camilla's first. I haven't eaten since lunch at your grandmother's."

If he'd forget about her project by the time they got back, she could keep their good-nights confined to the front porch.

He placed his hand atop hers. "Then let's do something about that."

But as they started toward the door, Jake paused and bent to pick up a stray page that must have fallen from her desk. As he straightened, he glanced down at it. The muscles of his arm tensed and an icy wave washed through her as together they stared at the headlines.

Behind Bars At Last.

A photo highlighting a dapper-looking character shackled between two police officers took up the top third of the page. But farther down a smaller but clearly identifiable 1940s photo of Jake's grandfather illustrated the subheading. Mob Bookkeeper Takes Down Boss.

She reached for the paper, but he held it away from her.

"What is this?" Frowning, his eyes rapidly scanned the small type. "Is this a joke?"

He didn't know about his grandfather? Or was he a good actor?

"I was going to tell you, Jake, I—"

"Tell me what?" His troubled gaze reflected his confusion. He gave the page a shake. "This photo looks like my granddad."

Before she could respond, he pulled away from her and strode a few feet to the bed to stand staring down at the printouts. Emails from Ava. Newspaper articles from the Chicago trial. Information from genealogy websites. The article and picture announcing Tommy's and Dexter's enlistment.

He picked up the latter.

"I don't understand this. What's going on? That's clearly Granddad when he was younger, but this paper calls him Tommy O'Donner."

She approached him quietly. "I know."

He turned toward her, his voice strained. "I asked you, Macy, what's going on?"

"I'm sorry, Jake, but—" How could she soften the blow? No matter how she said it the truth wouldn't be taken well. Reading the pain and confusion in his eyes, she now harbored no further doubt that he'd been in the dark as to his grandfather's origins.

"But what?"

She clasped her suddenly cold hands together. "Your grandfather, the man you know as Dexter Smith, was not born Dexter Smith."

His brows shot up. "Come again?"

She gently placed her hand on his arm, hoping he'd see how it hurt her to tell him this. "Your grandfather was born Tommy O'Donner. He met and became fast friends with Dexter Canton Smith when they were raised together in an orphanage."

"What are you saying? They decided to switch names?"

She shook her head. "Dexter, the real Dexter, died at Pearl Harbor. Tommy—your grandfather—was there, too, and he returned severely wounded. Lost his eye."

"No." Jake's eyes darkened. "He was injured on the job. An explosion."

She motioned to the papers, her voice gentle. "It will take considerable reading for you to piece it together, Jake, but it's all here. Your grandfather was Tommy O'Donner."

Jaw clenched, he shuffled the headline story to the front of the papers he clutched and slapped it with the back of his hand. "You're telling me my granddad was a mobster? A criminal?"

Please, Lord, help me to soften this blow.

"Apparently," she said, endeavoring to keep her voice even, calming, "he was a bookkeeper for their business fronts."

Relief passed through his eyes. "He didn't know what he'd gotten into, right?"

How she wished she could give him that comfort. But she couldn't lie to him. "In reading the articles, it's clear that he knew. But he changed his mind about working for them after a co-worker came to an untimely end."

Jake pulled away. "None of this makes any sense.

You didn't know my granddad or you'd agree. There's been a mistake. No offense, but some journalist jumped to conclusions, didn't check their facts."

She pressed her lips together, trying to find the words that would help him understand. "I thought that, too, Jake. But the evidence is clear. It appears that after testifying at the trial, Tommy disappeared. But not many months later, Dexter Smith arrived in Canyon Springs. The next year he married your grandmother."

"No way. He was a good and kind man and a highly-respected member of the community. A leader in the church. A successful businessman."

"Yes, he came here a successful businessman, with money to start a company, money to invest. He was only in his early twenties in 1946. Where did an orphan raised in an orphanage get that kind of money?"

"His family was well-off. He came into the inheritance when he came of age." Jake spoke with confidence, but when his gaze collided with hers, his eyes narrowed. "Wait a minute. What are you saying? That my grandfather stole his best friend's identity and showed up here with mob money?"

"He was a bookkeeper for organized crime. Once he testified against his bosses, he knew he'd have to run in order to stay alive. The papers identified him by name and used his picture. There was no way he could stay in Chicago. Is it any wonder that he'd embezzle? Build himself a backup plan for a fresh start?"

Jake squeezed his eyes shut for a brief moment. "Macy, I realize you pride yourself on the integrity of journalism, but this is my grandfather we're talking about."

"I'm sorry, Jake. I know this is a lot to take in all at once. We've had a hard time getting our heads around it ourselves."

He cut her a sharp look. "We?"

"Ava. A friend in St. Louis who helps me with research."

"Research for your blog."

She swallowed, her gaze not leaving his. "Yes."

"You wrote a blog post on my grandfather?" He studied her with suspicion.

"I had no idea he was your grandfather until I saw his and Ginny's wedding portrait today."

His gaze hardened as he turned to look at her laptop, at the printouts scattered throughout the room. "You know who he is now and yet you're going to post a story on him?"

"I—"

He took a step toward her, crushing the printouts in his hand, his voice low. "You're going to smear my grandfather's name all over the country? Bring shame to my grandma and the whole town? Macy, do you have any idea how many people here got their start with a loan from Granddad? A job with his company? How many looked to him for advice, trusting they'd get an honest evaluation? A Christian perspective?"

She licked her lips. "I intended to talk to you first."

He gave a disbelieving laugh. "Maybe now you do. Now that I've caught you exploiting my family and my town to further your own ambitions. You didn't know he was my grandfather yesterday or last week or whenever you started this research, but you didn't rush back from lunch and throw this all away once you knew the truth, did you? You didn't even tell me what was going on until I saw the paper. You're using us as a stepping stone to snag that coveted television program, aren't you? Grinding us under your heel without a second thought."

"That's not true and you have no right to say that. I would never have posted this without talking to you. I would never betray you like that."

She brushed by him to gather the papers from the bed.

"We both know your track record proves otherwise. I'd thought, Macy, that we'd put that behind us. But when I show up at your door with roses, all you wanted was to keep me from seeing what you were doing. You hid your plans from me again, so you could get your scoop without my interference." He snatched the papers from her hands, his tone deadly in its flat, unemotional delivery. "So help me, Macy, if you publish this story, the next time you see me you'll wish you hadn't."

She stepped up to him, her chin lifting as she stared into the grimness of his eyes. He had no right to talk to her like that. None. "Let me tell you something, Mr. Talford. This isn't solely about my ambition, it's about yours, too."

He snorted. "That's ridiculous."

"You think so? Then think again. You are so self-righteous. So worried about the speck in someone else's eye that you can't see the log in your own." With satisfaction, she noted the shock that registered momentarily. "Oh, you may be concerned about your grandma. About the town. But you know what I think? I think you're mainly concerned about what this story will do to *you.* To your reputation. Your standing in the community. Your future in government service."

He glared at her, but instead of firing back a defense, he calmly gathered another handful of printouts before crossing the room. Grasping the doorknob, he paused to look at her.

She couldn't breathe. Couldn't swallow. Couldn't speak. She could only stare back at him, belatedly recognizing how her hateful words had wounded him.

"Jake—"

Glancing at the vase of roses, his jaw hardened. He pulled open the door and silently stepped into the hallway.

Then disappeared down the stairs.

Chapter Nineteen

As devastating as Macy's earlier betrayal had been, it was nothing compared to this. Jake groaned as he sat on the back steps the following morning, his head in his hands. The story about Granddad would kill Grandma. Possibly literally. How could she ever hold up her head in town again? What would people think of a man who'd stolen another's identity? Who'd very possibly brought stolen money into town and distributed it widely, in effect poisoning, contaminating, them all?

Maybe he could get hold of a judge over at the county seat. Get a temporary restraining order to stop Macy from publishing the blog post. But on what grounds? Any attempt to halt her would become a matter of public record. Word would get around. The story would eventually become public knowledge.

He had only one hope—that Macy would look deep into her heart and choose not to post it.

Was that even remotely likely? She'd said she intended to discuss it with him before posting it. But he'd ignored her, saying hurtful, accusatory things that confirmed he hadn't truly forgiven her, would never trust her. She'd come back at him with her own finger-pointing, catching him off guard. If she'd harbored any reservations whatsoever about posting the story, his reaction to it would certainly have pushed her over the brink.

Abe's warm little body pressed in close to him and he slung his arm around the dog. At least he could trust old Abe. Ironic, wasn't it, that if it hadn't been for Macy he'd never have brought the beagle home.

Jake gave the dog a squeeze, then both returned to the living room, where he'd sat up into the wee hours of the morning reading through the papers he'd commandeered from Macy. Staring down at where they still lay on the coffee table, he again dropped into the recliner. Then he raised himself slightly, feeling something uncomfortable beneath him. His jacket, with the ring still in the pocket.

He'd had such high hopes for last night, just as he had six years ago, the day that ended with him sending the ring box flying across the room. But he didn't have the energy to do that now. Instead, he pulled the velvet drawstring bag from the pocket and emptied the ring into the palm of his hand. The light from the single lamp next to the chair illuminated the dainty gold band and its faceted diamond.

How could he have been so wrong twice?

"I thought I heard God's voice, Abe." He brought

his fist up firmly to his chest. "Right here. Deep inside. Both times."

He turned the ring in his fingers, remembering his anticipation, the assurance, the hope his heart had held such a short time ago.

After their first breakup, it had taken years to again feel he was listening and responding to God's inner promptings. For far too long he hadn't trusted himself, couldn't trust that he was truly hearing from God when making decisions. Gradually, he'd regained that confidence, but now...

He placed the velvet bag on the coffee table, next to the stack of papers, then laid the ring on it. Reluctantly he reached for the printouts.

Page after page of confirming evidence that everything Macy had said was true. It didn't make any sense. None of it reflected the man he knew his granddad to be. And yet it was all there. The photos. The clippings. The census records. The pieces of the puzzle came together to form one ugly irrevocable conclusion.

Granddad had knowingly worked for organized crime.

According to the Chicago papers, he'd been a willing accomplice, at least initially. Only after a friend's body had washed up on the shore of Lake Michigan, a bullet through his head, did Tommy O'Donner have a change of heart. He hadn't immediately run to the authorities, though, but bided his time. Gathering evidence? Or siphoning off mob funds into his own pockets?

Jake sank more deeply into his chair, his heart aching. No, maybe he wasn't an extortionist or a hit man, but his grandfather had willingly lived on the fringes of mob society.

"How could you have done this, Granddad?" He stared, unseeing, at the raftered ceiling above him. "How could you have been a part of that? I've looked up to you ever since I was a little kid. How could you betray me like this?"

In fact, he'd idolized him, building his own character around who he believed his granddad to be, around the examples he set. He'd spent his entire life endeavoring to think ahead, to ask himself what would Granddad Smith do in this situation?

But his grandfather had withheld a secret. Lived a lie.

Abe drew near and Jake gave him a pat before tossing down the printouts and picking up the Bible on the table next to him. Had it been such a short time ago that he'd prayerfully decided it would be good for his grandma to meet Macy? He'd risen from that prayer time with a light and purpose-filled heart, his next steps appearing sure and God-directed.

How had it gone so wrong?

Not only had he been stunned to learn of Macy's intention to betray him once again, but her parting words cut deep. She accused him of being self-righteous. Accused him of being more concerned about how his grandfather's dark past would affect him personally than what the impact would be on his grandma and Canyon Springs.

He placed the Bible back on the table. Macy was only making excuses, trying to get herself off the hook by turning the tables on him. Well, he wasn't buying it. There was no question he cared more about how the news would affect his grandma than how it would affect him.

With a quick intake of breath, Jake abruptly straightened. Had grandma known the truth all along and agreed to keep her husband's secret? Or had he kept it from her? Knowing his granddad—or at least knowing him as he'd thought he had—if he believed anything might hurt his Ginny, he'd have kept it to himself. Even taking it to the grave.

Jake couldn't risk Grandma being blindsided by the news when it appeared in Macy's blog. The story hadn't posted this morning. But tomorrow? Her last day in Canyon Springs?

He glanced at his watch. He had enough time to get to Grandma's before a meeting in the mayor's office.

Macy smiled stiffly as the cheerful B and B owner refilled her breakfast coffee cup. She'd slept little, reliving the shock on Jake's face, his confusion, his anger.

She'd lashed out at him when she should have remained silent. His words had hurt her deeply, but her own ugly accusations had hung heavily over her head throughout the night. More than once she'd reached for her cell phone, only to set it down again. She could apologize, but that wouldn't change anything. She couldn't take the words back. Couldn't erase the pain from his eyes.

"I guess your time is wrapping up in Canyon Springs." Nancy set the coffeepot on a tray next to her, then without comment removed the barely touched omelet from where it sat in front of Macy. "We're going to miss you around here."

Stirring creamer and the contents of a sugar packet into her cup, Macy smiled an acknowledgment, belatedly remembering the mayor had asked her to stop by his office this morning. She didn't look forward to that, to his innocently inquisitive interrogation about her and Jake.

"I'm going to miss everyone, as well."

Some more than others.

"So where are you off to next?"

"After a few weeks on a break back home in St. Louis, I'll journey to a coal mining town in Montana. Or at least it used to be a thriving mining town before the mine shut down. Now the townspeople are attempting to create a new economic base."

Nancy nodded her approval. "Just like what you did for us with your blog coverage and the fundraiser, I'm sure your presence will play a role in that."

"I hope so." But unlike in the past, the thought of being on the road brought no flash of energy, no sense of purpose.

Sensing she wasn't in a talkative mood, Nancy moved off to another guest. Macy lifted her steaming cup for a sip but, despite the sweetener, it turned bitter in her mouth.

On top of the argument with Jake, a phone call from her sister first thing that morning reminded her that Vanessa was growing impatient. It was evident as well that Nicole couldn't understand why she hadn't posted "the story" yet. What was she waiting for?

Unfortunately, there wasn't time to research and write another story that would meet her sponsor's expectations. It would be the story of Jake's grandfather's blighted past. Or nothing.

Nothing meant she'd never rise above her current level. Oh, she could keep the blog, but the prospect of book and television deals would vanish. She'd lose the chance at the success she'd strived for, and that her family had always expected.

Surely Jake would eventually come to see how important the story was to her and agree to her posting it? But if she waited for that, it would be too late.

A faint tune in her purse alerted her to an incoming call.

Her mother.

Abandoning her coffee, she rose from the table and quickly made her way to the French doors, then onto the back patio, where the crisp beauty of the morning belied the debilitating sorrow deep inside her. "Good morning, Mom."

"I don't know if it is or not," her mother shot back. "You have one more day in that place and you still haven't posted the story you assured me you have. I talked to your sister a bit ago and she agrees you've been dragging your feet ever since you got to this Copper Springs place."

"It's Canyon Springs," Macy said quietly, slowly starting down a brick walkway in the walled backyard. Crocus and daffodils poked up from elevated garden beds. A maple's leaves unfurled a springtime green.

No butterflies yet.

"Honey, if you put this story out there, do you have any idea what this sponsor can do for your career? For your sister's? This is your dream, Macy, don't throw it away."

Her mother's words jolted.

Trina Colston had given up her own journalistic dream to start a family when she'd found herself unexpectedly pregnant with her first child. Four kids later, she'd never gotten back into the game and never failed to remind those around her of what she'd sacrificed. But couldn't Mom see that being a wife and raising her children had been an important part of life, too? A part of life her daughter was missing out on?

"Who is this Mr. Councilman you've been writing about anyway? The one who showed you around town. Who emceed the fund-raiser. That silly name keeps cropping up in the comments from your Canyon Springs readers, alluding to him having an interest in you."

"It's Jake," she said bluntly, tired of keeping her family in the dark. What was the point? They'd eventually find out. May as well get the backlash over with now.

"Jake? Jake who? Macy—" Then she halted. After a moment of silence, her words came softly, measured. "Do not tell me this is the same Jake who derailed you years ago."

"He didn't derail me." Not intentionally anyway. Although she'd been unable to recognize it at the time, she could now see how losing Jake subconsciously played a part in souring her on investigative journalism. He'd cared for her and she'd betrayed him, just as she was feeling pressured to do again.

"What is he doing there?" Her mother sounded outraged. "Did he track you down? Follow you?"

Macy moved farther down the walk, lifting her face to the sun's rays filtering through the ponderosas. "He lives here."

Her mother gasped, then her words came accusingly. "You knew that before you scheduled this trip, didn't you?"

"I didn't. I had no idea. He moved here after he left Missouri."

"Oh, Macy, honey, you can't allow him to hold you back this time. You've worked hard. Sacrificed. Didn't I tell you that a man who won't support you in the things you love isn't the man for you?"

Macy frowned, remembering Mom hammering that home more than once. But what was she really saying? That Dad had held her back? That he wasn't the man for her? Surely she didn't mean that—they were still happily married—weren't they? No, Mom had it wrong. Her own self-limiting thinking was what held her back. Once her kids graduated, she could have taken on freelance reporting assignments again. Instead, she'd chosen to stay in the shadows and live vicariously through her children's achievements.

Especially Macy's.

"Jake isn't trying to hold me back." And truly he wasn't, was he? In his eyes, this post that was splintering their lives wasn't about her career. It was about personal repercussions from a story about his grandfather, how it would affect his family's reputation. The town he loved. His own future.

"It's distressing," her mother continued, "to know you think so little of yourself that you're allowing him to influence you again. I never would have thought you'd permit that man to step back into your life."

"I'm not." She'd made certain of that.

"Then why aren't you publishing this story you claim to have?"

"Mom—"

"Just like the last time, that man will soon be long gone and the career path that you were on will be unsalvageable. In ruins. Momentum will be lost that can't be regained." Her mother let out an angry sigh. "I must say, Macy, I am extremely disappointed in you."

"Not nearly as much as I am, Mom." She paused. "I love you. I'll talk to you later."

Drained, numb, she shut off her phone and stood frozen in the middle of the B and B's backyard.

Whose dream is this—yours or your mother's?

Jake's words had angered her, but now she could see a grain of truth in them. Was leaping from a blog she loved to celebrity status her dream? Did she truly want to host a television show? Continue to travel alone and lonely until she went to the grave?

What did she really want the future to bring?

And most of all, what did God want it to be?

Chapter Twenty

It had been the hardest thing he'd ever done in his life.

Jake, sitting next to his grandma on her living room sofa, gave her soft, wrinkled hand a squeeze. "I'm sorry Gran, but I felt you needed to know before anyone else. I realized last night I don't have any idea what Macy will decide to do. But I'm not optimistic."

Grandma returned the squeeze. She'd been delighted when he'd appeared on her doorstep unexpectedly, determined to fix him breakfast, pour him a cup of coffee. But it wasn't long before the laughter in her eyes evaporated. She now looked drained, washed out. Old.

"It is what it is, Jake," she said softly, patting his hand as if he were the one in need of comforting. "You can't rewrite history. I admit it's strange to think I was married for sixty-five years to a man named Tommy O'Donner and never knew it."

"I'd hoped he'd told you long ago and that the two of you had chosen not to share it with the family."

She shook her head, a faint smile touching her lips. "No."

"I believe with all my heart he loved you. If he didn't tell you it was because he wanted to protect you, didn't want to burden you with his past." He gave her hand another squeeze. "Nevertheless, if this story goes out on the World Wide Web, you're going to be the one left to deal with the consequences of his decision."

She lifted her head, a spark lighting her eyes. "You think the Canyon Springs natives will rise up and drive me out of town?"

"Over my dead body. But you'll be the focus of a lot of confused and hurt feelings, Grandma. People will want to know what you knew all these years. They may feel deceived. I mean, the whole town loves you and Granddad."

"And why is it they should stop loving either of us now?"

Jake shrugged. "Everyone thought Granddad was this larger-than-life godly man. One of the town's benefactors. It's likely the money he invested in the community, shared so liberally, was siphoned off from a Chicago mob."

"He said he inherited it from well-to-do family."

"Gran," he secured his grip on her hand, "I don't know how long the term has been used, but members of organized crime often refer to themselves as 'family.'"

She gave a little snort of amusement. "They do, don't they."

"This will be a blow to a lot of folks. I know I grew up believing Granddad was the epitome of Christ-likeness. I looked up to him. Emulated him."

"And now you're humiliated. Embarrassed."

He nodded, knowing it was true. "It's bad enough for us to know this about him, but come tomorrow the whole world may find out."

"That's why we're not to put our faith in people, but in God alone, Jake. People, no matter how good they are, will often disappoint us." Grandma leaned toward him, her gaze intent, her voice increasingly firm. "But you can still admire your grandfather. You can still look up to him. What he did in his past later moved him to make a decision to give his life to God. You believe, don't you, that making Jesus your Lord and Savior washes away the deepest of stains?"

"Of course."

"The grandfather you knew was the product of a new Spirit planted in him, his life a testimony to God's goodness. There's no call to be ashamed of that new man, Jake."

"I loved him so much, Grandma."

"And you can still love him—and hold your head up, be proud to be his grandson."

Jake stared in silence at his hands holding those of his grandma, his heart aching for her. For himself. For Macy. *God forgive her, for she doesn't know what she's about to do.*

"Grandma, do you...do you think I'm overly ambitious? I mean, selfishly so?"

"Did someone say you were?"

"Macy. She said I care more about this story placing a blot on my political future than I care about how it will affect you and Canyon Springs."

"Do you agree with her?"

He slipped his hands from his grandmother's and got to his feet. Then he moved to the fireplace to lean against the mantle, his fingers instinctively seeking out Granddad's cross in his trouser pocket. "I can admit I have goals. Goals for myself, goals for Canyon Springs, goals for the state of Arizona. But I never thought of them as selfish ambitions."

"But her assessment troubles you."

"It has me beginning to question my motives. Am I an attorney, a city councilman, because I truly want to bring about good for everyone in the community or...or because I want to be admired and respected and loved as much as Granddad was?"

"You think that's what Macy was driving at?"

"I don't know. All I know is I'll never be the man Granddad was. The new man he was, I mean." He drew in a slow breath. "I never told you or Granddad this. I was too ashamed to. But when I was back in Missouri I forgot a prime rule of being an attorney. Confidentiality. I hadn't been retained to represent him, but a friend turned to me for advice. I unthinkingly shared that confidence with someone else, didn't think twice about it. And, well, it had devastating repercussions on the career of that friend. Destroyed our friendship."

If Grandma suspected the person he'd told was Macy, she didn't give any indication.

"So you felt as though you'd betrayed yourself. That you'd fallen short of your personal ideals. Compromised your integrity."

"Yes."

She moved to stand in front of him, her eyes filled with compassion. "Welcome to the club, Jake."

"What club?"

"The only person who never compromised his ideals was Jesus Christ himself. It doesn't make you a bad person just because you've fallen short of that standard. It just makes you human. You've always prided yourself on your high standards of personal conduct. Your honesty. Your integrity. Those were things you saw in your grandfather."

He blinked rapidly. "I did."

"I assure you those things won't go away because of something your granddad did almost seventy years ago. I'm more proud than you'll ever know that you strive to do your best, to uphold family honor. But I stand here today and tell you that you can stop being mad at yourself for something God forgave you for the first time you asked Him."

Jake nodded, the heaviness in his heart lifting somewhat. "He did, didn't He?"

"And you know, too—" Grandma's gaze held his "—that no matter what Macy does, you'll need to forgive her, as well."

The heaviness settled in once again. "I hope and pray, Gran, that's something I won't be called on to do."

"I'm glad you could gather with me today," Gus Gustoffsen said as he smiled at the handful of council members, the president of the chamber of commerce—and Macy. "I won't take up a lot of your time as I know you have business to take care of on a weekday."

To Macy's disappointment, across the conference table from her Jake avoided meeting her eye, his attention focused solely on the mayor standing beside her.

Jake looked so handsome this morning, but tired. He probably hadn't slept any better than she had. No doubt he'd checked out her blog that morning and seen that she'd posted a lighthearted recap of the past month. But as they were both aware, there was one more post to come, the finale that everyone looked forward to with such anticipation. It could open the door to her future—and seal Jake's heart closed.

No, his heart had already been sealed. He didn't trust her. Never would. Why couldn't she accept that and get on with her life? She had only to hit the publish key and be done with the struggle, move forward into a bright and beautiful future. Never look back.

"Tomorrow is Macy's final day in Canyon Springs," the mayor continued, "and I want to acknowledge the favorable publicity she's provided for us. As Al here can attest, she's opened the floodgates to phone calls and emails seeking information about our dynamic mountain community."

Al nodded assurance that Gus was speaking the truth.

"Local shops and restaurants are reporting an increase in foot traffic for this time of year, too," Larry James added. "And Merle Perslow says calls to his real estate office for rental and purchase inquiries have increased significantly."

"With that said—" Gus picked up a framed document from the table and held it out for everyone to see. "I want to officially thank you, Macy, and present you with this certificate making you an honorary citizen of Canyon Springs."

She stood to receive it, but it wasn't the moment of happy triumph she often experienced when accepting sincere thanks from one of her *Hometowns With Heart*. Nevertheless, she was determined none there that morning would be the wiser. "I'm the one who should be thanking all of you—and the members of the community—who've made me feel welcome."

"Some more than others." Don guffawed and elbowed Jake. She winced inwardly as Jake put on a smile. When she'd entered the mayor's office, she'd overheard one council member whispering to another that they expected to see an engagement announcement in the final blog. She'd be returning to her own real world tomorrow evening, but Jake would be here to face the curious stares and the speculation as to what went wrong in their relationship.

Of course, if she published the story tomorrow, they wouldn't have to wonder, would they?

"I can honestly say this has been a wonderful month," she continued with an enthusiasm she didn't feel. "I don't know when I've felt so at home in such a short length of time."

The gratified guests beamed back at her, all except Jake, but she kept her own smile steady. "I will cherish my memories of Canyon Springs forever."

"You'll be coming back, won't you, Macy?" Larry cut a quick, questioning look in Jake's direction. "We'd sure hate to see you walk out of our lives. Become a stranger."

"Oh, I could never be a stranger, Larry. I'm only a blog post away. Leave a comment on it or email me off-line and I'll answer. I promise."

He didn't look satisfied with her response, nor did the others. Jake's expression remained neutral. Had they truly assumed she and Jake would make a match? That she'd throw her career away and settle down with them? It was wonderful to feel loved, but it wasn't the love of a *town* she craved...

"You've made this an amazing visit," she finished up, acutely aware of Jake. "I'm proud to be an honorary citizen of your fine community. Thank you."

The men and women clapped. Even Jake. Then

they all rose from their seats and came around the table to shake her hand and say a few parting words. All except Jake, who'd retreated to the bank of windows overlooking Main Street.

"I have another meeting across town," Gus said, mopping his brow. "But can I give you a big hug, Macy?"

She laughed. "I insist, Mr. Mayor."

He bent down and enveloped her in his arms with a hearty squeeze, then he straightened and cast Jake an uncertain glance. "I'll let this gentleman see you out. Thanks again, Macy, for all you've done for us."

When Gus and the others had departed, she cautiously approached Jake, moving to his side to look down at Main Street, as well. "You have a great hometown, Jake."

"I won't dispute that."

He'd obviously stuck around because he had something to say to her. She wished he'd spit it out and get it over with. Once he was finished, no matter how scathing his words, she'd apologize for her own harsh words of last night. For whatever that was worth.

He glanced over at her. "You didn't post the story this morning."

"No."

He folded his arms in a defensive motion. "Are you still planning to?"

"I'm…" She started to lift her hand to touch his muscled arm, then drew back. "It's possible my entire future rides on this post, Jake. I know you don't believe me, but I had no idea when I started it that Dexter-Tommy was your grandfather. I plan to go see your grandmother today. I wouldn't want anything posted without her being aware of it."

"Please don't. I already talked to her."

Her eyes searched his. "Did she know?"

She'd wondered that so often after meeting her at lunch, a lunch that seemed as if it had taken place a hundred years ago.

"No, she didn't." He turned to again stare out the window. "She said she'd long sensed there was something he wasn't telling her, something about his past that troubled him. But she never pushed him to talk about it. He'd given his life to God before they married and, as she puts it, he was clean and shiny bright before his Heavenly Father. A new man."

"How did…how did she take it?"

He gave a slight shake of his head. "Grandma's not one given to big displays of emotion, so it's hard to tell. She did say 'it is what it is.'"

"I guess that's one way of putting it."

Casting Macy a bleak look, he placed his hands to the sides of her upper arms and gently moved her a step out of his way. "Take care, Macy."

He strode to the door.

"Jake."

He halted, but didn't turn.

"I'm sorry." For what? For what she'd done to him six years ago? For what she was about to do to him, his grandmother, his town? Or for falling in love with him?

"Me, too."

And then he was gone.

Chapter Twenty-One

❧

You can't fight city hall.

The classic words echoed through his mind as he sat listening to the informal chitchat around the dinner table at Larry's house that night. He'd had his say. Expressed his opinions. And now it sounded as though at next week's council meeting the others would be voting against retaining his granddad's property. Nothing personal, they just needed to put the funds the property would bring to good use without delay.

On a brighter note, Larry had pulled him aside earlier to mention he'd be officially nominating him for appointment as vice mayor and expected a unanimous decision. As gratifying as that should be, with the loss of the property and tomorrow's blog finale looming over his head, it was an empty victory.

"Pass those mashed potatoes, please, would you, Jake?" Don said. "Unless you intend to keep them all to yourself."

"Sorry." He handed the bowl across the table, then took a sip of iced tea before retreating back into his thoughts.

Would Macy post the story tomorrow morning? For a moment she sounded as if she was undecided, but then she said she wanted to speak to his grandma. Why would she need to do that if she didn't intend to post it? She'd said she was sorry, too. For what? For what she was about to do to the whole town? To him?

The attorney in him demanded to confront her, to eloquently present his case a final time, to try to bend her to his will. But at the mayor's office he hadn't attempted to sway her. He was tired of fighting for what he thought was right. Tired of trying to make things go his way. Trying to control the outcome of every situation that challenged him.

"You'd better grab a piece, Jake, before Hector and his missus think you've gone vegan." Bernie's husband held out the platter of Hector's wife's fried chicken and Jake helped himself, although he wasn't hungry.

Mercifully, no one had mentioned Macy or tried to pry into the outcome of that relationship. It was probably pretty evident at this morning's gathering that any intrusive questions wouldn't be welcome. He couldn't blame them, though, for having hoped Macy would have a reason to stick around. They loved her. They liked him, too. What better ending to a month-long visit by a nationally known, popular blogger than to match them up and start ringing wedding bells? You couldn't pay enough for publicity like that.

Jake glanced around the table at his friends and colleagues, grateful for their support and sensitivity. He hated letting them down. Goodness knows, if everything had gone as he'd expected Macy would be sitting beside him right this minute, showing off that diamond ring. He'd be grinning ear to ear and when the two of them finally slipped away after the meal, he'd make sure the evening ended with a kiss she'd never forget.

At least they didn't seem upset with him for letting them down, letting Macy slip away. Listening to the good-natured chatter around the table, however, he couldn't help but wonder how they'd feel about him tomorrow. About his granddad. They couldn't help but look at him differently, could they? Think about him differently? Wonder if the apple might not fall too far from the tree?

He'd be glad to get it over with. The suspense, the dread of not knowing what Macy would do was almost more than he could bear.

An uneasiness roiled in his midsection. But what if Macy didn't post the story tomorrow? What if she *never* did? Could he gratefully accept that gift or would it eat away at him, always wondering when someone else would stumble across his grandfather's shortcomings? It could happen on the eve of his election as Canyon Springs's mayor. Or the night he threw his hat in the ring to run for state representative.

In retrospect, was it any surprise Granddad had never run for public office despite decades of urging? He had to have feared the truth would be discovered.

If it didn't come out now, would it later as Dexter-Tommy's grandson worked his way toward higher avenues of public service and people got snoopier about his background? He'd always be on guard, wary, looking over his shoulder, knowing that some political opponent could research his family and attempt to use it against him.

Even worse, what if it was learned he knew of his grandfather's shady history and concealed it? As long as the truth was a skeleton hanging in the closet, could he retain the self-respect and sense of family honor that, until now, he'd built around what he'd perceived of his grandfather's life?

He again gazed slowly around the table. He genuinely cared for his community, for the people he represented. With only a moment's hesitation, he abruptly stood. Conversation around him halted as everyone turned to look up at him curiously.

He cleared his throat. "I'm sorry to interrupt, but I have something I need to share with you...."

At the knock on her door, Macy glanced at her watch. Ten o'clock. A little late for a cookies and milk delivery. She rose from her desk, where she'd been polishing her latest post. She had to wrap it up soon. It would go out in a few hours.

A quick look through the peephole sent her stomach churning. Jake. What was he doing here? Suddenly short of breath, she momentarily closed her eyes. *Please, God...*

Reluctantly, she opened the door.

Jake stood there stiffly, his expression unreadable. "May I come in?"

She stepped back as he entered, then closed the door behind him. There was no point in other B and B guests being a party to this.

He slipped his hands into his trouser pockets. "I didn't want our last meeting to be the one in Gus's office this morning."

So he was here to say goodbye. "Thank you. I felt badly about that, as well."

He glanced at the vase of roses still sitting on the little table just inside the door. "I'm here to ask your forgiveness. And I want you to know I won't stand in your way of publishing the story about my granddad."

He was giving her permission to use the post? To win her sponsor's approval?

"Jake, I—"

He raised his hand to halt her. "I won't try to stop you by any legal means, so you won't see me in court. You won't ever have to see me again if you don't want to. But—" He moved to her desk, glancing down at the still-open post on her laptop screen. "I'd like to see the story beforehand."

"I'm not publishing it."

She'd already decided that this afternoon.

He raised a brow, confusion clouding his eyes. "You're free to post it, Macy. I've prayerfully thought over what you brought to my attention about my own ambitious motives. I've also come to realize not publishing it will haunt more than doing so. Most of all, publishing it will allow you to snag a TV pilot. A book deal. Achieve your dream."

"But your grandma…"

"I talked to her again tonight. She reconfirmed that Granddad's past is what made him who he was, what brought him to the Lord. She refuses to be ashamed of God's work."

"And the town?"

"I've met informally with the city council, gave chamber members and a few pastors a call. They unanimously gave the go-ahead to relay to you their approval. You've been good to Canyon Springs and they're excited about the opportunities awaiting you if this story pleases your sponsor."

She bit her lower lip, troubled. "What about you, Jake?"

He exhaled slowly, the corners of his mouth turning up slightly. "I'm good with it. Maybe Granddad's changed life will encourage others who feel stuck where they are to give God a chance, too." He nodded toward the laptop. "Like I said, though, I'd like to read it before you publish it."

She stepped between him and the computer. "No."

He frowned.

"I mean no, I can't publish it. I've prayed about it,

too, and I can't. I've written a substitute post for to-morrow. It won't make my sponsor happy, but I can live with that. You were right, I've allowed my family's expectations to weigh in on my life decisions for too long."

He remained silent, his gazed fixed on her as if he hadn't heard a word she'd said. "Let me see it, Macy. Please."

She didn't want him to see it. Yes, it was well written. She'd put her heart into it, emphasizing the man young Tommy had grown to be. How he'd put the past behind him and started fresh with his eyes on God. The story had become even more personal, more intimate knowing Tommy was Jake's grand-father.

Reluctantly, she closed the draft she'd been working on and pulled up the original post. It was longer than usual, illustrated with photos she'd gotten permission to use from the old newspapers. Swallowing hard, she moved away to allow Jake to read it in private.

When he finally finished, he stepped back. "Well done."

She motioned to the laptop. "Thank you, but like I said, I'm not publishing it. I won't do this to you. I respect you far too much."

He tilted his head to the side. "You'd refrain from posting this because you *respect* me?"

"Yes."

Moving to the vase, he pulled out a single rose.

Then he ducked his head slightly and hesitantly held it out to her. "I'd rather it be because you love me."

An electric shock raced through her as she stared at him. Was he saying what she thought he was saying?

He took a step toward her. "I've never stopped loving you, Macy. I know I didn't do things right. I didn't put my feelings in words. I didn't make a commitment. But I'm laying it on the line now. I… love…you."

She reached out an unsteady hand to take the rose from him, but before she could verbally respond, he'd dipped into his jacket pocket and pulled out a small velvet drawstring bag. Then he gently emptied it into his palm.

A diamond ring.

He gazed down at it almost reverentially, then at her. "I've had this ring a long time. Six years to be exact. But I couldn't bring myself to dispose of it."

"You bought this for me? Before—?"

He nodded. "I know I've made a lot of mistakes for which I need your forgiveness. I don't have all the answers. I don't know how we're going to work this out. The logistics, I mean, with you traveling and doing a TV program. Me practicing law in Canyon Springs and, God willing, working my way to the state capitol. But I'll compromise. I'll fly to wherever you are for a few days each week or a whole week each month. Or every other week. Whatever it takes."

Tears pricked her eyes. "Oh, Jake, I don't know how I could have missed it, spending a month in small town after small town, year after year."

"Missed what?"

"That I belong in a small town, too."

Uncertainty flickered through his eyes. "But the TV program. Your blog."

"I don't want to be on TV with a camera following me around, making people uncomfortable talking to me. I don't want to turn my blog into a tabloid. But I *can* write it based from anywhere that's within driving distance of an airport, including Canyon Springs."

"You'll lose your primary sponsor if you don't give them what they want from you."

"I can get another one."

He lifted a brow. "I take that to mean you love me, too?"

"Yes," she whispered, her heart pounding. "I always have and I always will."

"You'll marry me?"

"I will."

He stepped in closer and took her left hand gently in his, then slipped the ring onto her finger. Breaking into a grin he scooped her into his arms and dipped her back dramatically.

Prepared for a mind-blowing kiss, she belatedly realized he was reaching around her, his hand outstretched to her laptop. And before she could stop him, he selected "publish now."

The story about his grandfather—the good and the bad—sailed out to the World Wide Web.

Epilogue

"Look at you two," the mayor greeted them from the steps of Dexter and Ginny Smith's first home in Canyon Springs. He openly eyeballed their clasped hands with approval as they approached. "I can't tell you how proud I am for planting the idea of a courtship in Jake's head."

Jake didn't argue, letting him take credit. Instead, he shot a conspiratorial smile at Macy, then turned back to Gus. "So what did you want to see us about this morning?"

"I thought this would be an appropriate spot to let you know the city council members won't be asking for a vote to sell this place to the highest bidder."

Jake glanced at Macy, but she didn't seem to know where Gus was heading with this either. "So what's the plan now?"

"As you've probably heard," Gus continued, hardly able to suppress his excitement, "after that story hit Macy's blog last week, the business owners in town started vying to play up the Chicago mob angle to their advantage. The historical society thought it appropriate to make sure visitors to the community have an opportunity to know who Dex really was, not only the infamous aspects."

Macy squeezed Jake's hand. She'd told him she'd been beside herself with worry when Kit's Lodge added a half pound "mobster" steak burger as a weekly special—"not to order this would be a crime." Likewise, midweek sale ads popped up with 1940s car illustrations and touted "gangbuster bargains." Even the local pizzeria that specialized in the thin crust variety suddenly offered a Chicago-style deep dish.

Gus's smile broadened. "So they contacted the gentleman who'd assisted with the historical museum last year. This place is just down the street from there and would make a perfect museum annex. He agreed, so a sale will soon be final."

Jake's spirits soared, hardly believing what he was hearing.

"And…" Gus's smile teased. "It's unanimously agreed to dedicate one of the rooms to Dexter 'Tommy O'Donner' Smith. It will not only highlight his, shall we say, colorful past before coming to Canyon Springs, but everything he's done for the community since then."

"Are you serious?"

Gus nodded. "The historical society wants that book of yours on the museum's shelves, too."

"It's at the printer as we speak." Jake grinned at Macy. He'd rewritten the chapter on his grandparents—touching on Granddad's orphan past, his wartime service and, of course, his involvement in organized crime and the role he'd played in bringing several crime bosses to justice.

"That's a wonderful idea, Gus." Macy released Jake's hand, then ran up the steps to give the mayor a hug.

Although Jake had repeatedly reassured her that he didn't mind, she'd been appalled at how fast the town embraced its organized crime connection. But as he'd told her, the newness of the marketing campaign would probably wear off, fade away as many had in the past. By the end of summer, it would play out and they'd be looking for something new to catch the attention of next season's customers. What *would* last would be the support the town had shown to Jake and his grandmother, and the peace of mind they felt knowing that the secrets of the past had been laid to rest.

Gus, still blushing from Macy's enthusiastic embrace, glanced at his watch. "Well, I have to run. But I couldn't wait any longer to share the news."

As Gus hurried off, Jake joined Macy on the front porch, where she slipped her arms around his neck.

"Nobody's going to tear this place down, Jake. Or turn it into a tattoo parlor. Your grandfather's past will be commemorated in a tasteful way—beyond a mobster burger."

Jake laughed. It was amazing how few negative repercussions had come from Macy's post. Oh sure, a few clucked their tongues disapprovingly when it made the six o'clock Phoenix news. And a few local jokesters held their hands up and backed off when he met them on the street. A local vintage clothing shop owner had sneaked up behind him after church and popped a 1940s fedora on his head. But even Grandma was enjoying the attention that gave her the opportunity to tell people how God had changed her husband's life.

Macy gazed up at him happily. "You'd said you didn't know how things would work out for us. But I'd say it's pretty clear that God has a plan. Just look at the fact that my sponsor still wants me to write *Hometowns With Heart* books. They didn't even change their minds when I refused to change the tone of the blog or agree to a television program."

He grinned and pulled her closer. "I'm sure the overwhelming response to the online engagement announcement caught their attention. It all but put Granddad's story in the shadows. And your promising to post the details of our upcoming nuptials made your sponsor realize a Canyon Springs wedding is sure to boost readership."

Macy playfully poked him in the chest. "It didn't hurt, either, Mr. Councilman, that I posted your handsome face all over my blog. I think you could successfully start your own blog as a spinoff. From the comments I received, you've already built quite a following."

"Uh, I think I'll pass, thanks."

She snuggled in closer and his heart warmed. "I get the impression my sponsor would be happy if we had a lengthy engagement and played up the wedding for as long as we can."

"I'll go along with that. For a while anyway." He tightened his grip on her waist. "But I have my limits."

"Oh, you do, do you?" she said coyly.

For a long moment they gazed into each other's eyes. Then securing his arm behind her, he dipped her back for a kiss filled with promises he intended to keep.

* * * * *

Dear Reader,

Like any real-life couple, Jake and Macy faced challenges that often seemed insurmountable. But God used those challenges to develop their character and draw them closer to Him—and to each other.

In any relationship, there are frequent opportunities to "look not only to your own interests but also to the interests of others." When they first met, Macy and Jake were blind to those opportunities as well as to how their backgrounds and previous experiences influenced their beliefs and actions. Years later they received the gift of a second chance, but they had to acquire over time the ability to listen to God and develop the desire and strength to respond as He would ask.

I'm genuinely enjoying writing about the lives and loves of those who call Canyon Springs home, and I'm thrilled that so many of you have written to let me know this Arizona mountain town holds a special place in your heart, too!

I love hearing from readers, so please contact me via email at glynna@glynnakaye.com or Love Inspired Books, 233 Broadway, Suite 1001, New York, NY 10279. Please visit my website at glynnakaye. com—and stop by loveinspiredauthors.com, seekerville.net and seekerville.blogspot.com!

Glynna

Questions for Discussion

1. Jake's parents divorced when he was small and at a young age he stepped in as "the man of the family." How might this have developed his protective instincts, serious outlook on life and need to always make the "right" decision? What are the pros and cons of these attributes?

2. Macy comes from a family of high achievers and confides in Jake that as a professional blogger she's "the black sheep." How do you think Macy's feelings of being an outsider in her own family affect her personal and professional choices on a daily basis?

3. How do you think Jake's growing up years may have played a role in his choice of profession and desire for public service? What needs in him might achievements in these areas meet? How do you think God may lead Jake to satisfy these needs in a relationship with Him?

4. Jake's father abdicated his responsibilities as a husband and parent and Jake's stepfather also let him down. How do you think this magnified Jake's sensitivity to issues of trust?

5. Macy's mother's "lost opportunities" caused her to live vicariously through her daughter, remind-

ing her to "stop chasing butterflies." In order to achieve even God-given goals, it's necessary not only to trust Him but to work faithfully as He leads. Do you think there is ever a time for chasing butterflies? Why or why not? How is this similar to "stop and smell the roses?"

6. Why do you think Jake kept the engagement ring when he knew another woman wouldn't want a ring intended for a previous love? Why might he feel a need to be symbolically reminded of Macy's betrayal of his trust? Do you think keeping it was a spiritually healthy or unhealthy decision? Why?

7. Jake doesn't tell anyone he previously knew Macy because he's afraid they might learn he'd betrayed a confidence. Why do you think the incident from years ago still controls him now? Is there a failure to be perfect in your own past that has become amplified and affects how you perceive yourself today? A failure for which you know you are forgiven, but you haven't forgiven yourself? How might you accept and internalize God's forgiveness?

8. Macy's mother is deeply disappointed when Macy turns to blogging on human interest stories rather than investigative reporting. But when she sees the potential for the blog to become "some-

thing big," her pressure on Macy increases. How is this unhealthy for both mother and daughter? Do you think she may truly have her daughter's best interests at heart? Why or why not? How might this relationship be made whole and healthy?

9. Jake carries in his pocket a remembrance that his grandfather had also carried. Do you have any symbolic objects, verses or sayings that serve as a frequent reminder that God is in control and you need to put your trust in Him? Why is it so easy to forget?

10. One of the reasons Jake delayed speaking up when he believed Macy to be "the one" was that he wanted to be certain of a go-ahead from God. What are some Biblical guidelines people can follow to know when they have God's approval on a decision? Do you think if he'd spoken up years ago that he and Macy would have had a happily ever after? Why or why not?

11. When Macy learns that her break-out story will again betray Jake, she's devastated. Why do you think we often must face the same or similar challenges again and again? Has that ever happened to you?

12. Why couldn't Jake see the core motivation of his own ambitions, but focused on the negative

aspects of the ambitions of others? Discuss how the Biblical admonition to remove the log from our own eye before trying to take the speck out of someone else's eye might apply. What logs might you need to remove?

13. Do you think Macy made the right career decision at the conclusion of the story or do you think she will someday come to regret it? Explain your thoughts.

14. Despite the risks, Jake makes an irrevocable decision that could potentially affect his future and how others perceive him and his family. Do you think he made the right decision? What else might he have chosen to do? How do you think this will affect him on down the road?

15. Given the expectations of Macy's family and the dysfunctional father-son relationship in Jake's background, what challenges can Macy and Jake expect to face as a married couple? As parents? How might they, with God's help, overcome them?

LARGER-PRINT BOOKS!

GET 2 FREE
LARGER-PRINT NOVELS
PLUS 2 FREE
MYSTERY GIFTS

Love Inspired®

Larger-print novels are now available...

Reader Service.com

Manage your account online!
- Review your order history
- Manage your payments
- Update your address

---

*We've designed
the Harlequin® Reader Service
website just for you.*

Enjoy all the features!
- Reader excerpts from any series
- Respond to mailings and special monthly offers
- Discover new series available to you
- Browse the Bonus Bucks catalog
- Share your feedback

Visit us at:
ReaderService.com

LARGER-PRINT BOOKS!

GET 2 FREE LARGER-PRINT NOVELS PLUS 2 FREE MYSTERY GIFTS

Love Inspired® SUSPENSE
RIVETING INSPIRATIONAL ROMANCE

Larger-print novels are now available...

YES! Please send me 2 FREE LARGER-PRINT Love Inspired® Suspense novels and my 2 FREE mystery gifts (gifts are worth about $10). After receiving them, if I don't wish to receive any more books, I can return the shipping statement marked "cancel." If I don't cancel, I will receive 4 brand-new novels every month and be billed just $5.24 per book in the U.S. or $5.74 per book in Canada. That's a savings of at least 23% off the cover price. It's quite a bargain! Shipping and handling is just 50¢ per book in the U.S. and 75¢ per book in Canada.* I understand that accepting the 2 free books and gifts places me under no obligation to buy anything. I can always return a shipment and cancel at any time. Even if I never buy another book, the two free books and gifts are mine to keep forever.

110/310 IDN F5CC

Name	(PLEASE PRINT)	
Address		Apt. #
City	State/Prov.	Zip/Postal Code

Signature (if under 18, a parent or guardian must sign)

Mail to the Harlequin® Reader Service:
IN U.S.A.: P.O. Box 1867, Buffalo, NY 14240-1867
IN CANADA: P.O. Box 609, Fort Erie, Ontario L2A 5X3

Are you a current subscriber to Love Inspired Suspense books and want to receive the larger-print edition?
Call 1-800-873-8635 or visit www.ReaderService.com.

* Terms and prices subject to change without notice. Prices do not include applicable taxes. Sales tax applicable in N.Y. Canadian residents will be charged applicable taxes. Offer not valid in Quebec. This offer is limited to one order per household. Not valid for current subscribers to Love Inspired Suspense larger-print books. All orders subject to credit approval. Credit or debit balances in a customer's account(s) may be offset by any other outstanding balance owed by or to the customer. Please allow 4 to 6 weeks for delivery. Offer available while quantities last.

Your Privacy—The Harlequin® Reader Service is committed to protecting your privacy. Our Privacy Policy is available online at www.ReaderService.com or upon request from the Harlequin Reader Service.

We make a portion of our mailing list available to reputable third parties that offer products we believe may interest you. If you prefer that we not exchange your name with third parties, or if you wish to clarify or modify your communication preferences, please visit us at www.ReaderService.com/consumerchoice or write to us at Harlequin Reader Service Preference Service, P.O. Box 9062, Buffalo, NY 14269. Include your complete name and address.

LISLPDIR13R